Volume 1

The Irascible Pedagogue

The Silent Mistress

Requiem for Ernie

A Shotgun Wedding

A Dog Named Bunny

Woodsmoke

by Hilton Everett Moore

North of Nelson
by Hilton Everett Moore

Copyright 2022
Hilton Everett Moore
all rights reserved

Requiem for Ernie and *A Dog Named Bunny*
previously published in the U.P. Reader Spring of 2021

The Silent Mistress previously published by Illinois State University's
online publication "Euphemism" Fall of 2020
awarded Editor's Choice

Published by Silver Mountain Press
Covington, MI 49919

Printed by
Silver Mountain Press
Covington, MI 49919
ISBN 978-1-7367449-0-1 paperback
ISBN 978-1-7367449-2-5 hardcover

September 2022

www.writerinthewilderness.com
www.silvermountainpress.com

Cover & illustration by Andreea Chele

No portion of this publication may be reproduced, reprinted, or otherwise
copied for distribution purposes without the express written permission of
the author and publisher. For information address Silver Mountain Press,
P.O. Box 63, Covington, MI 49919

This is a work of fiction. Names, characters, business, events, locales and incidents are
the products of the author's imagination. Any resemblance to actual persons, living or
dead, or actual events or locales is purely coincidental.

Contents

Foreword   5

Acknowledgements   7

Timeline   9

The Irascible Pedagogue   13

The Silent Mistress   33

Requiem for Ernie   59

A Shotgun Wedding   77

A Dog Named Bunny   103

Woodsmoke   129

Foreword

This collection of short stories reflects upon the rich, rural culture and character of the Upper Peninsula of Michigan. The culture of the U.P. has been examined by such notable writers as Robert Traver (John Volker), Ernest Hemingway, Jim Harrison, John Smolens, and many others. These literary giants, much like Atlas, have carried on their solid and formidable shoulders this unique ground, and truthfully, I do not want to "mess" with these big guys. I only hope to build upon what they have already written. The scope of this work is to bring the reader closer to the ground: to examine, enlighten, and envelop this unique exposition of the U.P. in a way that perhaps the reader has not been exposed to before.

While the stories in this collection are set in an area "North of Nelson," the characters and events could just as easily have been set in any underserved and underdeveloped rural area of the United States; their universal themes are not confined by geography.

Acknowledgements

To an honest critic wherever she may be.

Grateful acknowledgement is made to the following:

Robert Boldrey – Always there for support and willingness to read whatever was too raw for general consumption.

Tina Vance – Meritorious efforts above and beyond the call of duty.

Timeline

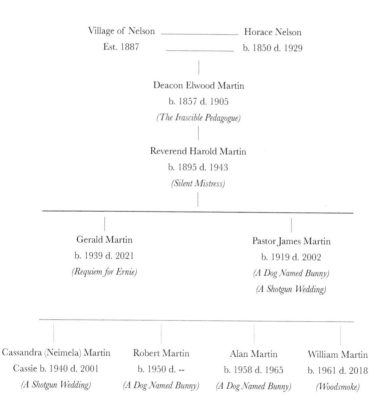

"Sometimes when the diaphanous moonlight filters through the iron bars of my cell, I think I see Lilith's visage."

I

The Irascible Pedagogue

It was the year 1881. Lilith, like many of her female friends and acquaintances, felt that with the onset of the suffrage movement, perhaps women would be allowed to have a new, welcome sense of freedom. Unbeknownst to Lilith, the right to vote and other rights freely given to men, were not inalienable, nor preordained by God or by legislative fiat. No, even the right to vote would be far in the future: the 19th Amendment would not become law until 1920.

She was, in her younger years, quite naïve and impulsive, as if the world should turn on her whims. I knew her then. There was also a slight touch of arrogance in her demeanor which was, I suppose, partly due to her attractive countenance. Though one might have suspected differently of a young woman raised in the rude rural culture of the Upper Peninsula, her flaws in character were present even in her youth and would grow and fester, much to my dismay. Lilith was a student at the one room school which I was assigned in this desolate area. And, as she matured into womanhood, she shed her naiveté much like her chemise; but later.

The nascent feminist movement must have given her a giddy sense of liberation which those around her, myself included, found disconcerting. She had a keen, but inelegant intellect and once had told me privately that perhaps females were finding a place in the world beyond the oppressive domain of men. I expect she felt heartened by that thought. I was appalled at her attitude but made light of the matter, not wanting to reveal my growing desire for her while still hoping that she might come around to a proper sense of decorum produced by the able hand of a sensible man. Maybe this newly discovered freedom, built on illusion, I would suggest, is what caused her, on that first lonely evening, to partially undress in front of her bedroom window— with the curtain open, naturally. The one who witnessed this most indelicate disrobing wasn't her carefree and cocksure husband, James, who was at a Grange Hall meeting. No, indeed no, she reserved this silent exposure for me, a bachelor pedagogue and her former fiancé.

My name is Horace Nelson, or as I always instructed my pupils to call me, Professor Nelson. I lived directly up the hill from Lilith, actually a stone's throw away, in a small, but tidy yellow clapboard house.

It was apparent to all who knew the exacting details of our former relationship that I had built this house on the crest of the hill overlooking her farmstead, not out of indifference, but out of a sense of spite. After many long decades I can admit to myself that, yes, that was the case. I suspect that Lilith might have candidly admitted to herself—with some minor reservations, mind you—that she had thrown me off, the rather ill-suited pedagogue, for her future husband, James. In truth, I believe that Lilith was impressed by his very pastoral and profitable farm, filled with plump cattle and all manner of produce, hay, and potatoes that grew abundantly on this most productive farm in the area. I suppose that James' choice of fertile ground was propitious, while neighbors barely scratched a living: though I am not deceived by superstition, I wondered if James' success was the proverbial luck of an Irishman. But upon much later reflection, I wondered if it was providence, as his reward would not be in this world. Regardless, my assumption was that Lilith did not see her betrothal to James as mercenary, but perhaps more as practical, but I would beg to differ.

I am certain that in the immediate distance she could see my shadowy silhouette, standing there in the smoky kerosene lamplight of my stark bedroom, and felt my uncomfortable stare. That first night I felt as if I were committing a nefarious act of some sort. But no, this temptress probably laughed out loud to herself. I recall, as if it were yesterday, when she stood facing my window, illuminated by the eerie light of the moon, which seemed to drift around her comely visage like an errant cloud. Lilith let one strap of her rose-colored chemise drift off her shoulder, revealing her full round breast. "Horace, look and be aroused," I could almost hear her say. She turned away in what I thought was a deliberate sensuous display, her back to the window, and blew out the lamp, as if extinguishing not only the light but my immediate temptations as well.

In late autumn, James was at another "meeting" and had left her alone, as was often the case. In the flickering lamplight Lilith taunted me again, as if amused by my deepest longings. Shamelessly, she turned away seductively from the window and in the dim light stepped out of her chemise. She must have thought that the gentle curve of her hips and the small of her back might entice even me, a normally stolid man to warm emotion. I was certain some inner need must have compelled her to do so, leaving me bereft and breathless and having to quench my own carnal desire.

Lilith must have imagined, and rightfully so, that I stared in a sort of awe, trying to envisage what would come next, and over an agonizing period of months she revealed to me more than I could have ever craved. Toward winter, one moon filled evening, I gazed at her in the soft light of the lamp as she slowly undressed; she opened the curtain as if she were turning the page in an alluring French novel. Fully disrobed, she stood facing me, then doused the sensuous flickering lamp.

I am certain that Lilith must have felt aroused and that perhaps any man would have provided her with relief, together, the smell of musk, intoxicating; alone—but I am certain in her mind, not alone. She must have sighed, as women in these times were wont to do.

I was in my early thirties when I escorted Lilith to the portentous fall dance at the Grange Hall. She had been the brightest student I had ever instructed in the miserable one-room schoolhouse. But perhaps that wasn't really much to be admired given the closeness of the nearby Ojibwe Indian Reservation whose children spoke in their unintelligible native tongue and had immense difficulty even mastering basic English skills. That, and the ill-bred immigrants that flooded this godforsaken place most of whom were unequipped intellectually to be anything but wretched miners, destitute farmers, or filthy itinerant loggers for the many deplorable logging camps. Regardless, the beautiful and intelligent Lilith was an exception and made up for the sundry others I was required to instruct. She had wished to read Les Misérables in French, a request which required a significant effort and fortuitously allowed us to engage in private after-school tutorials. She was an able student and easily advanced. Like the coming of an electrical storm, we would casually touch, all in the manner of educational pursuit, of course. That is until she reached for my hand one day, and as she applied her lips to my face, Lilith, astonishingly, placed my hand on her right breast. I quickly retracted my hand, flummoxed. "Lilith, we must not, unless, and until, we become engaged."

I had fallen astray once before and I had paid dearly; I did not wish to make that same mistake again. I wrenched inside, weighing my immediate carnal desires for Lilith against my possible ruination if our behavior ever became public.

"I really don't see marriage as necessary," she said matter-of-factly. "But I will agree, at least for the time being."

And that was how it all began. I gave her a ring with the caveat that she must not display this token in public. Patiently, I related to her that this ring was not an engagement ring but a possible sign of my future intentions—after a suitable period of time. I was uncertain what I wanted or needed from Lilith, as I knew that to reintroduce myself to respectable society in the East, Lilith would never be viewed as anything more than as a rural curiosity. She asked for clarity of my intentions but I demurred, relating that time was our ally and that we must wait for matrimony until my future was more clearly defined. At least that was what I implied. I churned internally, caught in my own vortex. Lilith expressed, with some unhappiness, that she felt I had left her in a quandary, not clear of what I intended. The calamitous dance came later.

On the Saturday of the dance, out of the corner of my eye I quietly watched her sip a cup of punch—sans alcohol, as the Grange Hall encouraged the temperance movement sweeping the country. I cringed as a fiddler scratched out an off-key waltz by Strauss.

She was just sixteen and had recently finished her education at my schoolhouse. She had hoped to matriculate to a university in lower Michigan, an admirable and lofty desire, and not unexpected for a young woman from a prosperous family. Though her family possessed adequate means for her to have an advanced education, she seemed to falter at the prospect, perhaps a feminine fear of the unknown. I hadn't encouraged her, not because she wasn't bright enough; no, that wasn't the case at all. As time went by it became clear to me that my unsaid intention was to seduce her, and a lofty degree of some sort was not needed for my sordid intentions.

I admitted, but only to myself, that a proper society marriage was necessary to eliminate the stain of expulsion that had occurred at Yale. I shuddered, remembering the formal charge of moral turpitude with a very young and precocious lass, just thirteen, the daughter of my headmaster. The charge finished my career. This blemish—that is what I silently called it—was the cause of my downfall as a budding professor of French Literature and my subsequent inability to obtain a professorship anywhere in the country. I knew my banishment was a rebuke that I could only cure by demonstrating strict moral behavior—and an ill step such as marrying the young and lovely Lilith would not be my first step back to civilization and redemption, but a faux pas. Furthermore, my desire to return to the East and comfortable society with Lilith, a country coquette, was not possible, as she would be a millstone around my neck. No, I would need a woman of proper breeding and sophistication. I longed for the time when I would no longer have to endure the intellectual wasteland of the Upper Peninsula of Michigan.

"Would you dance with me please?" Lilith cooed. "I so love Strauss, don't you, Horace?"

She wore a charming blue dress that fit her pleasant form nicely. I recall that when she was a young student, I thought she was without guile and false pretensions, but later that dreaded evening, I would change my opinion and seal my fate forever.

"Should we take a stroll down the road? Alone?" she asked softly. "There is an old oak tree there that would be a fine place to spend an hour or two—alone."

I observed that Deacon Elwood Martin from the Evangelical Lutheran Church was casting a glance in my direction, which made me anxious, so I gently declined. It wasn't that I didn't desire her; actually, I ached for her, but the invitation would need a more appropriate time. A misstep would ruin my plans.

Lilith, perhaps irritated at my refusal, told me with a hint of sarcasm, that she thought I was almost gallant for a starched collar pedagogue. I knew myself to be anything other than gallant; in truth, I was gloomy and dispirited and rather clumsy at the display of affection; I was dark, in both manner and countenance. This seemed a rather backhanded compliment at best and an insult at worst.

She laughed with an edge in her voice. "You remind me somewhat of Ichabod Crane."

Picturing that black-garbed scarecrow of a schoolmaster, I felt offended. Still, I could see her point.

"A dance, please?" she asked.

Angered by her slight, I replied, "I'm really a poor example of proper footwork, two left feet." I was aware that Deacon Martin was present, and that this stoic parishioner frowned on dancing of any sort. Elwood was also the president of the school board, such as it was in this illiterate county, and so I chose to not have a conflict with him; I always refrained from controversy if possible. Deacon Martin would become my nemeses, but that was later.

"Sorry, Lilith."

"I will have to find another partner then," she remarked coyly.

"As you please, my dear. After all, it is only a dance."

I was to realize later that my words were more than fateful.

Despite accepting the ring I had given her; she danced and she danced, with a young man named James, a handsome, displaced Irishman who grew tons of potatoes on his fertile farm. I desperately wanted to rebuke Lilith, but had no chance. She left the dance with James, and my fate was sealed. Lilith married James in the following spring. She never gave the ring back, which I decided resentfully was part of the female character. Though the ring was an inexpensive purchase, the refusal to return it rankled me. I am convinced that character arises from what we are exposed to. I think it is of note that Lilith was the only child of a prosperous local lumber merchant who often traveled to Detroit and Chicago and pampered her with gifts and foreign novels, from which the young and impressionable women drank deeply. It is difficult to dismiss the craven effects that these influences must have had on Lilith's character.

Lilith must have felt, a year after her marriage and the subsequent death of her young infant, that time parcels out opportunities begrudgingly. In my own life I have come to the conclusion that what initially looks like a boon, often over time is revealed as a bane. While I agreed that the world is dark and barbaric as Deacon Martin suggested in many of his simpleminded sermons—we could ill-afford a parson willing to take a charge in this desolate county—I felt compelled to listen to his inarticulate ramblings. Short and stout, and expelling spit on the unfortunate souls in the front row of the rudely crafted church, he did not exude anything like the fiery oratory of a Jonathan Edwards, despite this poor man's pretentions. Though Deacon Elwood was my junior by slight years he always fostered a paternalistic attitude toward me which I found particularly irritating and condescending. I have come to the conclusion that most dabbling poets and simpleminded deacons deliver pabulum only fit for the likes of children.

I knew from gossip that James, though purportedly a patient and loving man, drank to excess. After the end of his long days tending cattle and working assiduously in the potato and hay fields, he would harness up his buggy and head several miles down the road to the local tavern. From my porch window I was able to observe that James rarely came home early, unless, I assume, it was to grope Lillith like a mating ape, which I am sure she found unacceptable.

Once a month James attended the Grange Hall meetings and was, as far as I knew, a competent officer, though I later found out that his meetings were really romantic liaisons with a female in the organization. The following year Lilith confided to a mutual neighbor that she had come to accept the difficulties and the faithlessness of her husband as well. From my vantage point on the crest of the hill, I was delighted, certain that Lilith felt gentle stirrings for me that she could not easily resolve.

At the time of her marriage, I had been gravely wounded and embarrassed by Lilith's public rejection, and although the two of us never spoke of it, I grieved, which was a personal revelation to me. I was certain that she should have been betrothed to me, and that I had been betrayed. As if in almost direct opposition to Lilith's marriage to James, I resolved to be wedded to the wretched northern wilderness, angrily giving up entirely my dream to regain decent society in the East.

I was later to regret this decision.

I can't extinguish a night that is branded into my brain, as if a hot poker seared my very flesh. Through the window I stared in disgust as James, drunk I suppose, ripped Lilith's chemise from her slight frame. At first, she seemed to resist, but later, perhaps in defiance of her husband, Lilith appeared to return his forced desire with a sense of intimate, but violent sensual pleasure. I remain revolted both by her husband's crude advances and later, by Lilith's worldly response.

As time wore on, perhaps she experienced a seething anger, and that is what impelled her to return partially naked to her bedroom window. Over a period of time, she seductively undressed for me in the dimming light. This seduction was almost a sequential affair, as initially she would only show one breast, which filled my senses like a smoldering ember. In truth, I coveted what James so cavalierly cast aside. As time went by, the blackness of my mind assaulted me and I ached; later she would uncover both breasts before dousing the lamp.

In my mind I could almost hear her whisperings: "Horace, come watch. I am still capable of quenching the fire of your loins." I imagined she said these words softly in French to my shadow up the hill. Unable to divert my eyes, I felt obsessed with diametrically opposing feelings. I harbored both a need for diminution of my pleasurable longings and at the same time I felt a sense of repulsive guilt. Why did I covet her so? To this day I wonder.

Sometimes the raw passage of time resolves issues of the heart; and sometimes not. Gradually I became inflamed with jealousy, which was not assuaged by either time or the carnal desire I felt for Lilith. It was not pleasure that inhabited my mind, but anger, and ultimately, outrage. For a brief period, Lilith suspended her naked displays, which drove me further to despair. Later, after several months of modest propriety she again returned to her window and resumed her wanton displays, I deeply suspected for my benefit. This vacillation between her need for vulgar display on the one hand, and on the other a compulsive need for discretion drove my mind, like a raging torrent, to disgust at her depravity.

While initially I had not wanted her, had she not been promised to me? Chosen me? Was she not taunting me, revealing her all to me? I believed that she was my lover, even though this desire had never been consummated. In retrospect, the situation of all involved might have been predictable, as the jealousy I felt was putrefying and spreading—an infection I harbored like an untreatable disease, a building craze that I seemed incapable of reversing.

One night, as James staggered drunk out of the tavern, I attacked him with my cane.

"James, you animal!" I shouted as I beat him about the chest. Though James was short in stature, he was well-muscled from farm labor. James tried to stem the blows and fought back as well as he could in his drunken state. A cut above my eye opened and blood streamed down my face. I was enraged and struck back again. He stumbled, and fell to the ground as patrons of the tavern, poured out hearing the clamor.

"You have ruined her, you swine! I shouted as I raised the cane again. "You have stolen her innocence and replaced it with filth!"

The cudgel rained down on James again, cracking his skull like a broken melon. James lay quivering unable to rise. I took a step back, horrified at my own baseness. Several farmers came to wrestle me to the ground, pinning me and tying my wrists with a harness until the Sheriff arrived.

A crowd gathered at the scene, and I was promptly arrested and later tried for attempted murder. James survived, but was a mere shadow of the man he was before. Deacon Elwood Martin testified at my trial that I had a flawed character as I had on occasion questioned the sanctity of Holy Communion, which as an agnostic was accurate, but hardly a worthwhile argument in a legal proceeding. While this religious indictment seemed inconsequential to me, it was relevant to the mostly pious jury of uneducated dullards in this village. I was found guilty of aggravated assault and received a sentence of twenty years of hard labor with a possible chance of parole, given good behavior.

James, or what remained of the broken man, required a lengthy hospitalization. He was later confined to bed in their homestead, where he lapsed into a permanent coma and had to be ministered to night and day by Lilith.

While in solitary confinement, I was later told by a guard that her invalid husband lay unconscious in the marital bed near the window. One might hope that this was the ending of this traumatic triad, but that was not the case. For after a long period, perhaps two years or more, Lilith, exhausted by her role as a constant and obligatory caregiver, informed his doctor that James had passed. My silent speculation to this day is that she had smothered James with a pillow. It was reported she remained mute at the inquest, and the coroner ruled that her husband's demise probably resulted from injuries from my vicious attack. Shortly after James' death I was retried for second degree murder despite my attorney's insistence that the charge was a case of double jeopardy, a legal guarantee which is provided for in the constitution. Deacon Martin, curse his soul, once again testified against me and I was found guilty and received a life sentence without the chance for parole.

Lilith sold the profitable farm for cash, a most propitious move, considering that the entire farm economy collapsed in the Panic of 1893. She sailed for France shortly after settling her affairs.

I only know the truth of Lilith's heartfelt confession of her husband's murder from a letter I received from one of her former lovers. According to this monsieur she had passed quietly in the town of Giverny, France, in 1897, twelve years after her husband's untimely demise at her own hands. Later, producing the damning letter to the court, implicating Lilith in her husband's death, I would argue vehemently for a retrial but was refused.

I still possess this lover's letter, as if in describing her state of mind I am able to exhume a work of buried art. This letter he sent, evidently a promise monsieur had made to Lilith shortly before her death, often keeps me awake at night in my dank cell. Lilith confided to him that she hoped the letter, a confession of sorts, might exonerate me for the death of her uncouth husband, for whom she had felt nothing but scorn.

The monsieur confided that Lilith had resided in relative comfort in the village of Giverny, a center for several great Impressionist artists at the time, including Monet. According to him, she was a frequent and welcome guest in homes of this influential group, and her gaiety and joie de vivre were highly regarded by her friends and associates. This monsieur wrote longingly of Lilith, a mutual feeling, I sadly admit I still carry. He related that Lilith was a most admired model and contributed to many artistic works. He wrote with a sense of passion—a deep and abiding longing, I presume. This man related that Lilith contributed mainly by modeling as a nude—of course, what else was I to assume? And that she had even posed for the likes of Degas and several other famous artists. Unfortunately, he lamented she had recently died from complications related to syphilis and was buried, per her request, without ceremony in the cemetery in Giverny.

I suppose the notorious nature of my crime, featured in the state's only prominent paper, the Detroit Free Press, captured the salacious interests of its readers. As I lay rotting in my prison cell, a village sprang up around the old schoolhouse where I had formerly taught, a putrid curse of sorts, as the village became known as Nelson, for my now-infamous surname. Now in advanced years, I garden for the warden, tending his flowers—yes flowers—and his many rosebushes which fill my days and bring some small comfort.

In the prison darkness, sometimes when the diaphanous moonlight filters through the iron bars of my cell, I think I see Lilith's visage as she steps out of her nightgown—and I weep, wishing I had taken the offer to dance—it was only a foolish dance played badly by a scratchy fiddler. Now I grieve wishing I had taken her, possessed her as she had urged me to do. Oh, the price of piety and most certainly, prison, the penance for stupidity.

"Sometimes in the dark of the night, I wonder why I stayed with Charlie."

~ II ~

The Silent Mistress

I toss another shovel of dirt onto Charlie's casket as the young priest looks on. I didn't ask the priest to be here, and in fact resented his presence, but he had informed me that all burials at the cemetery must be consecrated. The priest looked resentful too, as if Charlie, my mate of roughly thirty years, deserved to die for giving up on his faith. I don't try to tell the arrogant priest that Charlie knew God, in his own way, and often told me he could hear his presence in the swaying branches of a red oak or the rattle of a rutting buck scraping on a popple sapling.

I pause and lean on the shovel, remembering, as the priest walks away—disgruntled, I imagine, because another soul was not saved. Or perhaps the priest is rejecting me for my native blood and because as a young woman I ran away from the orphanage and left the church.

It would be pleasant to assume that our first night at Charlie's place was romantic, but it wasn't. His place was a tar paper shack on Lake Baraga, on a back forty, down a muddy dead-end road, and it certainly didn't meet my image of a romantic place, or as Charlie might have said, "Tweren't romantic enough." I was just fifteen when I pulled off my chemise and stood there in the lamplight, expecting that Charlie, a young man the same age as me, would know what to do, but that wasn't the case. I remember that mostly we fumbled around in the dark, the dim light from the kerosene lantern making shadow-like specters on the wall. I had no idea what to expect, and as Charlie bashfully told me later, he had no idea either. We were both green as grass. I'm not sure where the white man's notion of love comes from, but in those first few years with Charlie, I sometimes couldn't stand him. I suppose cause we were dirt poor we stayed together out of necessity, each clinging close together like scab apples, blemishes in all, on the same darn withered tree. I guess some would call that love but I don't.

I had told the Father I didn't want the undertaker covering Charlie. I wanted to perform that task by myself. A blister swelled on the palm of my hand, but I carried on without complaint. The Catholic cemetery, here for over a century, was attached to the orphanage as if bound by an umbilical cord. In some ways little had changed in the church and the attached cemetery in the thirty or so years I had known Charlie.

Charlie and I were born in 1908. My life began in the squat brick orphanage in Baraga, while Charlie was born in a squalid logging camp somewhere to the east of the orphanage and north of the Village of Nelson, in the rugged Huron Mountains of the Upper Peninsula. My Native American mother brought me to the orphanage and stayed just long enough for my Christian naming, which the priest insisted upon; he gave me the name of Elizabeth, after St. Elizabeth I suppose, and so it was. It seems that St. Elizabeth, mother of John the Baptist, finally conceived at the ripe age of 60. The Catholic Church now accepts her as the patron saint of barren women. Ironically, I never conceived, and with Charlie dead, never will. The nuns, out of their ignorance or more likely their arrogance, promptly forgot my native name, which I later learned was Nimkii. That name, which I now prefer, roughly translates in English to Thunder. In my mother's tribe, Ojibwe, the name of a child is a sacred ceremony often initiated by a tribal elder. This sacred naming ceremony often takes place over a period of months if not years. I now believe my mother must have had a premonition that I would be like thunder rumbling across the Huron Mountains nearby, the comforting and fading echoes moving through the crags and granite cliffs signaling that the storm has passed. For the most part I am not intemperate, but as Charlie had learned the hard way over the many years you don't cross Thunder without consequences. Most of the pious nuns promptly forgot my mother's name as well, except for Sister Catherine, who spoke endearingly of her. As I grew older and better prepared for the truth, Sister Catherine told me that the year after my birth my young mother had quietly slipped into death from consumption.

The Catholic orphanage, squats next to the Red Stone St. Michael's church, high on the cold and windy shores of Lake Superior, a part of the state of Michigan that still remains remote and isolated. In my observation, Saint Michaels seems a fitting symbol for the strangling grip that Catholicism has inflicted on my Native race. This saint, often portrayed as a spiritual warrior, has often been associated with slaying the metaphorical dragon of Satan. My tribe's nearby reservation lies many miles from most anything of any importance, tucked tight to the land like a gnarled fist. Forests of mixed conifers and hardwoods surround the orphanage and line the rocky coast of Lake Superior. Much like the revered vestments of the local priest who ministered to the thirty or so children at the orphanage, the forests were a protecting but smothering presence that we all knew only too well.

I was not of age when Charlie Swanson and I ran off, but I was beginning what one nun once told me was the "ripening for God." I wasn't certain what she meant at the time, but now I understand she meant that with menstruation. I was, if willing, mature enough to become a nun. Fortunately, I didn't make that damn choice. Back then the very thought sent a shiver down my spine. I wanted nothing to do with the forced spinsterhood of the withered old ladies who ran the orphanage. When Charlie came along, I felt as if fate had interceded on my behalf.

Out of respect for his recently dead mother, one Sunday, Charlie attended mass. We didn't have a chance to speak that day, as I was required to sit with all the other orphan girls. He sat toward the back of the sanctuary as the priest droned on in Latin, unintelligible to most of us. Charlie was ill-dressed, with pant legs too short for his gangly frame, and he had a mop of stringy brown hair and one prominent gold front tooth which I would later learn came from a fight with a logger intent on raping his mother. True to camp law, the offending logger was later tied up to a pine tree by the crew and beaten near to death by the young boy with an oak axe handle. The offending logger was then promptly fired but not before the crew leader deducted a hefty fee for the itinerant dentist that sometimes showed up a couple times a year. Charlie got a new gold front tooth which he was proud of; he thought highly of the dental work. I kept my contrary opinions to myself. Charlie told me that the bloody logger vanished never to be seen again.

Looking back, I can't decide now whether Charlie caught my eye or I caught Charlie's. I guess the result was the same. After several weeks he passed me a note on which had been scribbled, "Pack your satchel and meet me at the church cemetery this afternoon—and don't tell no one."

I suppose I saw Charlie as an escape from the orphanage, as mostly Indians were only prepared for life as a domestic. While many of the young Indian women at the orphanage accepted this as their fate, I adamantly refused this life of imposed drudgery. If necessary, I would seek solace at the reservation. The only recompense I ever received from the damn orphanage was that I could read and write. I learned later that Charlie was illiterate and that a fellow he knew had egged him on about the pleasures of "having" a squaw. This friend had written the note in exchange for a bottle of beer.

The nuns regularly warned the girls of the evil sin of fornication, but Sister Catherine had, as always, privately counseled me that she thought otherwise. Quietly defiant of the priest who ruled over the half dozen nuns of the orphanage, the wizened old nun took a shine to me and became a trusted confidante. Sister Catherine once told me, with a smile, that women had private parts that they could use for pleasure, despite what the priest might say.

I loved this old nun like a mother. Sister Catherine, although a devout Catholic and directed not to do so, taught me the oral history of my people. She had learned the Ojibwe stories over the long course of her devoted life ministering to my people on the nearby reservation. Her tales were to become the foundation of my spiritual beliefs in the gifts of the Great Spirit and the power of Winabojo that guided me through the rest of my life. Sister Catherine patiently explained to me that in my native culture Winabojo was a spiritual being who represented all of the sentient creatures of the world, human, fauna, and flora, and was considered to be the master of all life. I asked her once why as a Catholic she became so interested in the native culture of the Ojibwe, "Well Nimkii, every human is a child of God and needs his care. I know my opinions could be called heresy but I put as much faith in your culture's view of God as Catholicism. If I am wrong then perhaps, I will spend my eternity in hell—but I will live my life according to my head and heart and damn the consequences." I was shocked by her very frank admission but strangely comforted as well. As I have aged, I have come to the conclusion that she was the most honest and courageous human I had ever met. Living with Charlie in the near-wilderness of the Upper Peninsula I was immersed in the power of nature and still remain in awe at what Winabojo has taught me over the course of my difficult life.

I hear the scrape of my shovel in the solemn and lonely cemetery and send a thankful prayer heavenward to both Charlie and Sister Catherine.

The nuns—except Sister Catherine, of course—treated me and the mostly native girls harshly, frequently rapping our knuckles with a stick as if our native blood was a curse that could only be restrained by brute force and not cured by examples of loving care. I hated the orphanage for what I felt it was, an article of Catholic torture, not much different than the tortures of hell that the church expounded on, and which the rigid nuns taught us were the justifiable consequence of worshiping the Great Spirit and not Christ.

In quiet opposition to the priest, Sister Catherine had told me of my parents and my tribal heritage, and most importantly of the power of the Indian Way. Sister Catherine told me in confidence that she had also been raised in a Catholic orphanage and regrettably had known no other way to make her way in life other than as a nun. She cautioned me not to make the same mistake. Despite suffering with consumption at an advanced age, she was often in conflict with the priest who requested the bishop to excommunicate her shortly before her death. Father Patrick, the parish priest, out of guilt I suspect for his request, let her finish out her life in the convent. While she was alive, she did what she could to shield me from some of the harsh penalties inflicted by several of the more unyielding nuns. But after Sister Catherine's death the other nuns at the orphanage made my life unbearable, as I was not easily broken to the yoke of Catholicism.

Charlie's grave is half full now. I rest for a spell, thinking. The orphanage is just up the hill, and this lonely cemetery reminds me of the holy Garden of Gethsemane. A large pine near the well-pump rises like a cross, but I wonder if the holy cross was the burden of a wandering Jew or an unlucky and broken Indian? As a young woman I would come here to pray before I'd enter the dreaded Catholic church.

I recall Sister Catherine's quiet revelations of my birth on the Ojibwe reservation to my mother, Aandeg, which means Crow. Sister Catherine told me that my birth to Aandeg had been difficult. According to Sister Catherine, Aandeg had taken up with a worthless, arrogant white who dealt in rot-gut whiskey and lived on the edge of the reservation. The chief had informed her she was welcome to bring up her child on the reservation but that my father was not welcome. Aandeg chose to leave, but died shortly thereafter.

What may seem to many as reckless, I now see as the workings of the Great Spirit. Of course, I met Charlie at the cemetery, as his note instructed. It was the year 1923, and that is how all the rest of my life began.

I scoop another shovel of dirt as I remember how the orphanage faded out of view in the pickup's Model A mirror on that warm July day. It felt as if the oppressive beliefs that had been forced upon me by the starched nuns, along with the rigid Catholic visage of Christ, also faded away in the rearview mirror. The muddy road to Charlie's place seemed to pull me, like the will of something much stronger than anything I had ever known—deep, deep into the wilderness. My Catholic beliefs never returned—and I thought at the time, good riddance to them.

The sun is closing on the horizon, a chill hung

in the air, and I must soon finish a task that a part of me wants never to be completed. The end of my labor seems to mark the end of a life I would like to hold onto and can't seem to release. Thoughts of Charlie crowd my mind. After Charlie and I "got together" we would often fish on Lake Baraga for bluegills. Most of the time he was a patient teacher, except when I lost a "biggun." We didn't have fancy rigs, just thin willow branches for poles and the usual hook and line. Charlie used to whittle out bobbers from a chunk of cedar.

Thinking back, I realize that life proceeds much without our knowing it. We go on doing all the duties of life, unaware that time is slipping away like a colorful bluegill, dangling on a hook and sliding through the hands of a careless fisherman. What could have been a certain meal becomes an opportunity missed. I guess I could have regrets. I read incessantly as books allowed me to evade my lot in life and the dire poverty and harsh life in the wilderness. My friend Emma would borrow books for me from the library in town when she went to the general store for supplies. I particularly liked the later and darker works by Twain, especially "Letters from The Earth" for instance. Tolstoy, Dostoevsky, and Poe also appealed to me I suppose because my world was often bleak and what I read just reflected the world I lived in. The library didn't loan books out to Indians. I had minimal formal education; my life was one of grinding poverty with an alcoholic; and sadly, no children graced my life. But through it all, I had Charlie. Life has not been so bad to me. Emma once remarked that I was "stoic" and that I should have left Charlie early on, but I drew her up short. "Damnit Emma the world of a half-breed is like living with a noose permanently tied around your neck waiting for some white bastard to kick the slats out from under you. My options are damn few and Charlie is the best I got. How would I support myself? Doing some rich man's laundry or emptying filthy bedpans? I care for Charlie, maybe I wouldn't call it love but life isn't perfect and he is the best I got going for me." Later that evening I sat and watched gratefully as Charlie rocked in his chair smoking a hand-rolled and I thought quietly to myself that perhaps the bluegill still ended up in the sizzling frying pan.

For all his faults Charlie was a humble boy who came from humble stock. I learned to appreciate this self-less man who, despite my misgivings often whittled wooden toys for the children at the orphanage. During the depths of the Depression, despite our own desperate circumstances, he would often drag home an unemployed logger or vagrant for a hot meal. He gave more to life than he ever took and he had no enemies, neither man nor beast. Often, he would feed the ever-present chickadees seed and whiskey in the harsh winter, watching them for hours through the kitchen window of the shack. On the rare sunny days when the snow piled deep, especially toward the end of his life, he would sit on the rickety porch on a cast-off rocking chair, feeding the gregarious birds. These flighty avians would alight on his shoulder and peck at the seeds from his hands, while some sipped Jack from a shot glass he had sitting on the railing. His face would fill with a gentle mirth as he watched the antics of the small birds. I suppose what I felt then was a sense of contentment that filled me up like a generous piece of sponge cake at a Grange Hall picnic. It wasn't as if I needed Charlie to feel complete, cause I didn't, but despite all our hardships, I appreciated this flawed man, and the next slice of yellow cake was like gettin' heaping seconds for nothing.

Charlie's mother worked as a cook in the logging camps, and Charlie, who had no idea who his father was, grew up with more than a passing acquaintance with the mean end of a crosscut saw, as if the saw was just another appendage that God thought a man needed to survive in this world.

The logging camp and all of the men there became kind of like a group of fathers to Charlie, and one of them probably was. They were a rough bunch who cussed, drank, and whored on Friday nights after they got paid. I guess it is sarcastic to say, but they were lousy examples as far as fathers were concerned.

Charlie built the shack out of saw ends; wasn't very pretty. Charlie had scraped away a meager amount for this cut-over forty sitting on the edge of a cedar swamp on the north side of Lake Baraga, miles from town. We rarely had a visitor, except maybe a misplaced hunter or the local parson's wife, Emma from the country church down the road. The modest clapboard church was the charge of Reverend Harold Martin who had become pastor after his father Deacon Elwood Martin had passed away, kinda' keepin' the preaching in the family, so to speak. The church was a half dozen miles north of Nelson. Emma, the parson's wife, who would stop by on occasion, always insisted I call her Sister Emma as if God would really give a damn about such things. Later, as Charlie got sicker, the itinerant doctor from Bishop would come around twice a year or so and check on him.

Despite our hardships, which were many, for years our life together was like the creek beside the cabin. The water flowed by without comment, as if to utter complaint was unnecessary. All in all, this wasn't so bad. Charlie worked in the woods for a local logging company, and I did the chores at home: cooking, washing, baking bread in the coal-oil stove, and chopping and stacking firewood for the long winters that hang on well past the spring equinox. This way we split our responsibilities. It was a quiet existence that was uninterrupted, for the most part, by the doings of the world—that is, until 1933, in the depths of the Depression, when Charlie lost his job in the woods and was unable to find work of any kind. That is when he started drinking at the country tavern in Nelson, the village closest to our shack. He'd always drink hard and on occasion I would even join him, though the tavern didn't like squaws in this shabby joint. In those days all us female natives were just called squaws, and though I was bothered by this derogatory name, I expected little more from the whites.

But all that was before Charlie started getting bad. It didn't take long before he had drunk up the money we had stashed in a mason jar we hid in the outhouse. Charlie stubbornly refused to go on the dole. A Republican, though he never voted, Charlie railed against what he believed was the downfall of America: FDR. I thought Charlie would come around to the New Deal, but he never did, and we sank into the financial abyss that haunted millions of others in the sorry state of the economy during the Depression. I know this seems sad, but we felt some small comfort that we were not alone in our misery.

It was the winter of '33, and I'd taken to snaring rabbits in the swamp. Charlie was cutting firewood to sell, piling the pickup high and overloaded to save money on gas. He told me often that he could fix that old truck with baling wire and a screwdriver, and he usually did. We eked out the bitter winter on fried flatbread, beans, and stewed rabbit, along with some stringy venison thrown in the cast iron pot. We had poached the venison out of season, and I had put it up in Mason bottles. One spring day the game warden stopped by, and I offered him a plate of venison stew. Charlie just grinned and put another forkful in his mouth. The game warden, I am sure the wiser, never uttered a word other than to thank me for the plate of "beef" stew.

One winter day late in the following February, Charlie remarked, "You're damn good at snaring rabbits, Lizzie. Who learned you that?"

"Read it in a book, Charlie, that the preacher woman, Sister Emma, lent me."

He watched as I carefully slit thin strips from a popple branch and soaked the strips in salt water to bait my wire snares. Though practically brought up in the woods, he had little time for woodcraft, having spent the bulk of his young life bucking wood and hauling water for his mother's needs at the logging camps.

"You know, you're damn good lookin' for an Indian," he once said with a chuckle.

"Thanks," I muttered, hurt and offended by his remark. Though I knew he was just teasing me, the words cut me, as if he were gutting a deer. I always measured myself against white women and found myself wanting. To be an Indian woman is to never be enough for any white man, and though I loved him, Charlie was no exception.

Smiling, he slid his hand under my flannel shirt and then scooped me up like a ragdoll and took me to bed. Later that evening he told me he was going to the tavern. I waited in the shadow of the lamp, the luminescence like a faltering omen, for his drunken return. I often wondered if he had another woman in his life, who he met at the tavern, and I quaked at the thought.

As I remember it was the year 1936 when FDR's phone lines came snaking through the rural countryside, connecting disparate folks like a heavy logging chain. The church folks quietly got together and paid for the installation of our phone line. The damned thing required a monthly payment, which I paid for by selling homemade bread at the weekly church bazaar; twenty-seven loaves or more. I still remember the smell from the fresh loaves piping hot from the coal-stove oven. The money I squirreled away in a mason jar, which I hid from Charlie so he wouldn't drink it up.

Sister Emma, the preacher's wife, called me. "Isn't this remarkable, Lizzie? Now we can talk more often."

I wasn't sure the newfangled device was a boon, as I rather like silence, but I admitted to myself that the device could be useful in an emergency.

"Yes, it's a wonder," I said flatly. Sister Emma was the closest friend I would ever have, though I didn't realize it at the time. "I suppose I can call the tavern now when Charlie's drunk and nag him to come home," I added sarcastically.

Sister Emma knew all about Charlie's "habit," but just thought that if Charlie would "find" Christ all of our woes would disappear. I knew better, but usually bit my tongue when she started proselytizing. She meant well. Sister Emma's husband, Reverend Harold Martin, the stiff-backed evangelical preacher of the backwoods congregation in Nelson, never visited. When I once asked Sister Emma the reason, she had implied that since Charlie and I weren't legally married, we lived in sin, and thus were a poison of sorts to the "saved." I tried not to hold my nose when she started on a rant, but sometimes it was damn hard. Most of the time I ignored the ring of the new thing hanging on the wall.

Sister Emma often showed up uninvited, which I became accustomed to over the years. She would arrive for "coffee," not distressed when I served her the ground-up chicory weed that grew in the ditches alongside the road. I would toast the weed, with the pretty cornflower blue petals, in the oven and grind it up with my old pepper mill. Sister Emma was a good soul, arriving with a plate of buttermilk cookies and several weeks'-worth of the local paper, which we could not afford to buy. In the evenings I would read Charlie the local news. The small-town paper had a smattering of world news, which always intrigued Charlie. He would listen attentively, when he wasn't drunk that is, and comment insightfully. He was what Sister Emma once described as "wood-wise, but book dumb." Maybe so, but he could spit snuff and argue with the best of 'em at the tavern.

'37 was a particularly hard year, what with Charlie's drinking hard liquor and no jobs. As his alcoholism worsened, he had given up drinking beer and moved to cheap whiskey. We lived on swamp buck, which tastes and smells much like the pungent cedar that those tough old bucks eat. We both turned twenty-nine that year, and despite trying, we had no children. I silently grieved, as I knew that time was not on my side.

"Don't worry, Lizzie, we'll have a brood before it's all over," Charlie said, nuzzling me one night. "I'm just holding out my bullets for the big un." I laughed despite hurting.

Charlie could make me feel that way, as if all our ordeals were insignificant and a dose of the dancing northern lights or a startling harvest moon could right our universe. I guess you could call that contentment, and despite his increased craving for drink, he seemed to take the sufferings of his world in stride.

When Charlie was at the tavern, I often cried myself to sleep. I miscarried in June that year, and for a while my world caved in around me like a waiting tomb, as if an undertaker was shoveling scoops of dirt on my chest, constricting my efforts to breathe.

Charlie complained of severe abdominal pain, and we traveled to Bishop to Old Doc Smithson's office. The doctor confirmed my suspicions—liver disease. Despite the doctor's recommendations, Charlie continued to drink. I begged him tearfully to stop, but almost in quiet defiance of life, his drinking increased. Late in the summer he found a job at a local sawmill, his first job in several years, and for a few months he seemed to recover his sense of self as he fought desperately to contain his near-fatal consumption of drink; but in the end he relapsed. He missed days at work and was rightfully fired. We went without again.

Sister Emma once offered to take me in, to save me, I suppose, from Charlie. But to save me from what? A life I had freely chosen? To save me for a white man's God I didn't know or, more accurately, I didn't care to know? I had rejected that world already and could never accept a God that allowed so much misery to exist: mine or anyone else's. If my fate was in my own hands, then so be it. The Great Spirit of my forefathers, the Indian Way, had been ripped from my soul at birth only to be replaced with a bitter God that shat on my people and my loved one. I had no use for the way of the whites, which I found foul and degrading to my true culture. Better to die with my head tilted toward the sun and the breath of the fecund earth in my lungs than to be strangled from above by the hands of a praying priest.

Charlie continued to drink as the last of our savings dwindled. We ate beans, only beans, and the occasional batch of flapjacks made from the sack of flour Sister Emma gave me. Charlie was too sick to poach a deer. I tried to hunt, but the bucks, like apparitions, faded into the swamps and eluded my efforts.

Sometimes in the dark of the night I wonder now, why I stayed with Charlie? Like so many in the Great Depression, we had nothing, but that was true of most everyone around here. I guess I hoped things would get better—someday.

It was 1936 and the season was changing, from the cold and drizzle of a wet fall to the advent of winter. Deep winter snows came early, and with it, desperation, like an unwelcome guest who meant to stay until death found us. Our money was gone. What remained was a bag of flour, crawling with weevils. We ate unleavened bread for lack of yeast. Charlie worsened.

At Christmastime, Sister Emma from the goodness of her soul arrived with children from the church to sing carols. The children had trudged through the snowdrifts on snowshoes as the winter winds had driven the snow to crests like frozen waves. The roads were virtually impassable and would be so for weeks. Sister Emma had filled a sleigh with boxes of food and treats for us, and we all sang carols as Charlie, lying sick in our bed, joined in, his voice strained from the effort. Sister Emma prayed with Charlie, and he seemed serene for the first time in months. After the group left, he held my hand, telling me he was ready for whatever came next—even Jesus calling for him to meet his maker. He fouled the bed that evening, and ashamed, cried.

In the quiet of the following evening, I stood in front of the cracked bureau mirror, the silvered edges faded with time. I was naked after having a sponge bath and could see the ravages of my life that my head and heart could not negate. My breasts now sagged like cedar boughs pressed down heavy with winter snow. The reflection revealed what time and culture could not deny. My round face and almond eyes were part and parcel of my mixed race, and no matter how I tried I would always be a squaw. Charlie awakened. Gazing intently at me, he grinned. "You know, Lizzie, you are the most beautiful woman I have ever seen—naked, that is. He smiled and rolled over in the bed and fell back to sleep. I laughed to myself, knowing he had told the truth and that the fact of the matter was that he had never seen another woman naked but me. It was at that moment that it dawned on me that I was terribly wrong, that in truth the only other mistress Charlie had known was the one that had always given him more than I could ever give; the one that had always seduced him and left him wanting for more, the enticingly familiar one: alcohol, or as the offending bitch is sometimes called, Miss Ethel.

Later Christmas evening he asked me to get a small box out of his jacket pocket. I wondered what this request was all about, but did as he wished. I handed the box to him, and he in return gave it back.

"This is for you, Lizzie," he wheezed.

I took the small box and opened it slowly. Inside was a gold ring—a simple but beautiful gold ring. "I don't need a ring, Charlie," I cried. He gently squeezed my hand.

"Where you get the money for the ring Charlie?"

"Well to tell you the truth Lizzie, last fall I sold the gold in my tooth—kinda' in advance to Old Doc Watson the dentist. You see, in exchange for the tooth Doc cast me up the ring. Course I had to throw in a load of dry, split firewood too. Didn't figure I would need that tooth after I was dead. But you gotta' promise me that after I die you will give that tooth up to Doc, you hear? A deal is a deal."

"Oh Charlie." A tear ran down my cheek. He smiled weakly and coughed. I slipped the ring on my finger as he rolled over and went to sleep.

Several weeks after Christmas the road was finally plowed, and Sister Emma picked me up in her auto.

The Silent Mistress

We made a necessary trip to town to sign up for the dole. Despite Charlie's objections I wasn't going to let us starve. I was never able to tell Charlie where the supplies had come from—though I was willing to lie to him that I had been sitting on some money I hadn't told him about, just for an emergency. All of that intended deceit was unnecessary.

Emma and I had been gone the entire day, and when we pulled into the drive, Charlie's bare legs were sticking out from underneath the Model A. Panicking I ran to the truck, hauled him close, and shook his prostrate form laying in the cold snow, already suspecting what had occurred. He was dead. Antifreeze drooled from the corner of his mouth. I pummeled his chest, moaning and crying in grief, aware that he had swallowed the deadly glycol, a mortal alcoholic alternative. Charlie made his own antifreeze from the drugstore glycerin, but it was deadly to drink. He had poisoned himself, either deliberately or perhaps not deliberately. I was never to understand his intent.

While I held and swayed Charlie's body, Sister Emma called Doc Smithson on my telephone, the sole medical practitioner in our county and also the coroner. After that she called the sheriff and agreed to meet him on the county line road and direct him to the shack, as he did not know where our place was located. Sister Emma cried softly with me, and then slowly drove away to meet the sheriff.

I lay down beside Charlie on the snowy ground

and shoved his body over crying, "Damnit, move over, Charlie. We've always done everything together, and we're not gonna' stop now." I moved under the radiator drain that held the glycol and opened the drain tap. The first sip was sweet, like honey. I drank deeply.

Fate often takes over where it wishes, pushing a person over, just like I'd done to Charlie's corpse, forcing life to go on even when you don't want it to. Old Doc Smithson, who was known to drink some, had a bottle of vodka in his car and forced me to swallow the damn contents. I don't agree with the lofty notion of divine intercession, but at that time vodka was the only known antidote to antifreeze poisoning. I gagged and vomited and was sick for some days afterward, but survived my own desire to die.

I lived on, but I will always have a part of me that is with my dead husband, Charlie: gifts of memories and a gift of love.

The grave filled, tired, I lean against the shovel and raise my head to the sky, wailing my people's ritual song of death. My song echoes in the near darkness of the graveyard, my voice quivering. In the wind I think I hear Charlie's voice quietly reply, "It's all right, Lizzie; it's all right."

I twist the ring on my finger; I know, I truly know, I will always wear his ring.

"My painful reflections that the world was small was just a compression of the larger world around me."

III

Requiem for Ernie

In 1953, a child's world seemed small in an isolated rural community on the rugged side of nowhere. Our nowhere was in Nelson, a small village standing in the shadows of the nearby Huron Mountains. At that time in my young life, I thought the mountains and scrub timber were imposing, but as I matured, I came to understand that the granite mountains had framed my younger years much like a theatre curtain to a proscenium, a necessary part of the backdrop of my unfolding life. It was as if the mountains were part of this unique drama, and the miles and miles of cutover cedar swamps and aspen, the characters in a play of my own design. The word rural doesn't define the area well; it was the "sticks". Times were tough there for the few folks with enough sisu, or spunk, as the Finnish immigrants put it, to labor in the woods and aging copper mines of the nearby Keweenaw Peninsula, a land of harsh storms sweeping off Lake Superior. As I look back, my painful reflection that the world was small was just a compression of the larger world around me, a necessity of sorts, to help me cope with life.

As I remember my early years, the corners are bent over like a faded photo, a difficult recollection in a grainy black and white memory, as my life was often beset by misery, I had polio.

When I write that my world seemed small, perhaps what I mean is constricted. It was a time when this country seemed innocent, but in truth, it wasn't small or innocent at all. America was on the cusp of violent change, but in my world all of this was as far away as the sailing ships I drew meticulously on notebook paper, plowing through cerulean waves on the South Seas. By the 1960s the country would convulse, but in 1953 these endemic problems seemed far away to a young boy, much like the final destination of the pulpwood and second cut hardwood that sat on the railroad sidings destined for belching paper mills far in the distance. The seemingly endless rows of pulpwood fueled much of the local economy, pulled either west or south by the huffing diesel trains, their heavy loads chugging by my house several times a day. Even at that young age I understood that the old growth timber had been logged off years ago, the land stripped bare of this valuable asset only to be replaced by the secondary pulp mill trade, a squeezing of the earth for profit that humans seemed incapable of stopping. Though I did not understand this process, the country was ripening with social pathology and would signal the end of life as I knew it. In long drives through the countryside, my father, a pastor and environmentalist before the word was coined, pointed out for my edification the exhausted landscape, mostly timbered over and dotted with fallow and deserted former homesteads, cast aside by failing farmers during the Great Depression. In some areas of this rural county the fallow land was left with pullulating plants intermixed with various weeds of all sorts: milkweed, sorrel, pigweed, and the like and the ever-present aspen. The worn land was only fit for hay crops to feed small herds of hardy cattle. Later in life it would occur to me that his symbolic regression of the landscape, as a succession of scrub and regrowth replaced the timbered-over land would alter this tired land for generations. A change in the environment was evident to all that cared to see. Eventually, the environmental and social issues, much like weeds, would suck precious moisture from the meager soil of a troubled society, but that would come later.

In some ways my life reflected the sorry state of the land around me. With polio, my life was hemmed in as much by social and psychological constraints as it was by physical constraints. In my mind the acres of scrub timber stretched far into the distance and seemed to me like penitentiary bars—and like a prisoner I felt confinement as a slow form of mental torture, though of course it was the actual polio that kept me imprisoned. I suppose it is equally difficult to explain how socially constraining polio was to me. At fourteen I was unable to play baseball with my younger, timid, and chubby friend Ernie because I wore the ubiquitous braces that were the curse of many a victim of this ravaging disease. Often in the quiet of my room I wept from loneliness. The braces made it difficult for me to navigate the stairs to my bedroom, and once there, exhausted by the climb, I would often play lonely games of solitaire until my persistent mother forced me to come down for a meal, and then the whole damn process would start again.

The infirmities of my disease left me consigned to stare longingly out the second-story window of my bedroom. The dusty, weed-infested ball diamond was across the street from our house and next to the train track, but it seemed to me a thousand miles away.

Mrs. Larsen's dilapidated house sat forlornly next to the ballfield. Bored, for hours at a time, I would watch her leghorn chickens pecking at worms and bugs on the ball diamond when the neighborhood kids weren't around to throw stones at these pesky creatures.

Dr. Jonas Salk announced the discovery of a vaccine for polio that year, but it was too late for me, and the transmission of polio was still an open question. Many families were rightfully frightened for their offspring. Afraid Ernie would catch the virus, his mother instructed him not to come next door to my house, although on occasion he would slip around to my back door and let himself in. My mother was complicit in this juvenile act and didn't admonish either Ernie or me. I could sincerely understand Ernie's mother's reluctance, though I will say, I was terribly alone. I remember my mother once remarked angrily, "Gerald, sometimes I hate God for what he has done to you. Nobody deserves your pain and suffering." Mother, felt her only son had been punished enough by God and wasn't going to inflict more pain by deliberately isolating me.

Lacking much else to do but to observe life, I became an interloper of sorts. Other than Ernie's occasional visits I spent my days daydreaming, watching glumly as the daily trains rumbled along the right-field fence of the old diamond, or watching sullenly as the neighborhood boys played baseball. Through my bay window spy-glass I studied the nuanced world of boys, where rules and a sense of fair play were not necessarily a given. Because Ernie was chubby, he was teased mercilessly, and I sometimes felt powerless to stop the distress he must have endured. At times it was as if he, too, was a victim of my imagined war, and I wanted him to feel as tortured by an enemy as I felt abused by my own condition. I understand now that my need to see Ernie as a fellow victim was morally wrong; but I was just a kid and have forgiven myself, but at the time I was lashing out at the world and couldn't see my own failings. Years later, I now feel a sense of shame for such a selfish need, but as a kid I felt we were brothers in pain and I often secretly gloated over his misery.

More than anything, though, we were good friends. But there was a gulf between Ernie and me that later in life I would recognize. Ernie's father was a soldier in the Marines and was stationed in Korea, a typical grunt, my father called him. My father, Reverend Harold Martin was the Methodist minister in Nelson, and had a dim view of the Korean Conflict, as that ugly war was euphemistically called. As a minister, he was highly regarded in our rural village, while Ernie's dad was considered by many to be a rough character. Ernie's father shot pool and drank to excess when he came home on leave.

I was a lonely child, with just one much older half-brother Henry, from my father's ill-fated marriage to Elinor; that disastrous arrangement was later annulled and only spoken of in hushed whispers by my parents. Interestingly, Henry, after seminary, would take up the ministerial robe and carry on the family tradition of pastoring the small congregation in Nelson, but more of that later. Ernie's house was always full of frenetic activity. I mentioned my envy of Ernie's many brothers and sisters to my mother, she just rolled her eyes and winked at my father, who was camped out on his favorite leather chair in the living room. He laid down his paper, bemused. My mother smiled and ruefully noted to my father that when Ernie's dad came home on leave, his harried wife was often left in the family way shortly after his departure. I was unsure of this adult humor and kept my best guesses to myself.

Even though Ernie had many siblings he would now be considered a loner. Regardless, Ernie's Catholic household's many children roamed around the village unpenned, much like Mrs. Larsen's laying hens, that scratched and pecked indiscriminately on the neighboring ballfield. After Ernie's mother's many complaints about chicken crap on her children's shoes, Mrs. Larsen reluctantly fenced the feathered offenders in her yard.

Often Ernie climbed the steep stairs of our old peeling clapboard house to my second-floor bedroom, we would talk baseball and swap baseball cards. I once traded him a dog-eared Mickey Mantle card for a pristine Rocky Colavito. We would spend hours reading and trading comic books and telling stupid jokes. I suppose I could say we were best friends. Ernie told me that his father had named him after the famous baseball announcer Ernie Harwell, who broadcast the games over their old Philco radio in the early forties. Ernie's father had promised his wife that they would name their next son Ernie as a tribute to the revered announcer. Evidently, she agreed, but no one was sure why. My friend Ernie had been born in 1943 when Harwell was broadcasting for the minor league team, the Atlanta Crackers. Ernie told me confidently while sitting on the edge of my bed that the Crackers won the league championship in 1946, when he was just three. His father credited Harwell's enthusiasm behind the microphone for the spectacular season the Crackers had. Ernie was genuinely proud of his name.

When Ernie's father was home on leave from Korea, they listened to baseball games on their radio—when the static wasn't too bad. Ernie Harwell was a honey-mouthed announcer who called the games in a slow, southern drawl that drew the listener in like a mesmerizing séance. Ernie used to beam with pleasure when he told me of the sultry late evening games that he and his father would listen to well into the summer's night.

As the conflict dragged on, Ernie's father had to go back to Korea. In my cloistered bedroom, Ernie and I listened intently to the games on the radio as Harwell, who had now jumped ship, was announcing for the New York Giants. Just before the Fourth of July, the Giants squared off against the Chicago Cubs. Harwell's voice was like butter left out on a warm day. While technically he was supposed to be announcing for the Giants, he seemed to our young ears to favor the Cubs, our underdog team. Later, we would change our slippery allegiance to our state team, the Detroit Tigers. Boys are like that.

Although Ernie Harwell was not hired by the Tigers until 1960, Ernie told me that in 1951 his father had written a letter to Walter O. Briggs Sr., the owner of the Tigers, suggesting that he hire Ernie Harwell as the Tigers' official announcer. He showed me the crumpled letter from Mr. Briggs Sr., pulling it from his dirty jean pocket, which confirmed that indeed, Mr. Briggs did value Ernie's father's suggestion and thanked his father for his keen baseball acumen, but at this time he had decided not to offer the job to Harwell, but perhaps later.

Some memories are like old chewing gum stuck tight under the seat of a baseball bleacher; they are difficult to extract. I remember watching from my bedroom window on early summer mornings, as Ernie played pretend baseball. Years ago, it was not unusual for a chubby ten-year-old with few friends to play pretend games. Maybe it is still that way, I don't know. I vividly recall one morning in mid-June, when the sun was low in the tentatively cloudy sky and the world was very quiet, watching Ernie from my window. The dew was heavy and wet on the weed-infested ball field, long before the local boys were up and going, and even before the morning train growled noisily past the ball diamond.

Unseen, I gazed from my open window and heard Ernie's throaty yell. "It's a solid hit for the right-hander," he said excitedly, in a voice that seemed to mimic Ernie Harwell. "It's headed for right field, and it could be a homer!" He ran as fast as his short, pudgy legs could manage, barreling around the bases: first, second, third, and then headed for home, jumping up and down on home plate, dust circling around his stocky frame, and yelling, "Hurrah, hurrah!" He sucked in gasps of air, exhausted by his efforts, and stood alone on home plate as if deciding what to do next. He repeated this same home run scenario several times till, almost painfully, he walked morosely over to the empty bleachers and sat down alone, as the sun arose crimson in the eastern sky. I will always recall watching him at this most private moment, and I felt as if I were intruding, but at the same time I felt compelled, drawn in by this most personal glimpse of another human being. He sat quietly on a broken bleacher and watched, as I did, the long, smoking diesel train trundle by, filled with pulpwood from the local logging outfit and headed to the papermill in Duluth, Minnesota.

Ernie sat forlornly on the bench. I recall he once had told me that he hoped to grow up to be a big-league ballplayer. It occurred to me at this poignant moment that perhaps he understood on some level this was a fiction he had dreamt up and that it was never to be. Ernie was perceptive in a simple childhood way and hinted to me one day that he was saddened beyond grief at this private revelation. Looking back, it seems remarkable that Ernie knew, even at that young age, that certain dreams are out of one's reach; but he did. Ernie's insightful observation was not news to me, as I had lived with disappointment my whole life, but I had always underestimated Ernie's insights. Ironically, my own pain often blocked me from feeling empathy.

Several days later, on April 14, 1953, and shortly before the Korean armistice, I watched from my bedroom window as two tall, sharply dressed Marines, one carrying a satchel, pulled up to Ernie's house in an official automobile and strode silently towards the porch. I gazed, sickened, from my window, as I knew intuitively that it would be a sad day for everyone in our small town. The Korean Conflict had claimed one of our own. My father delivered the eulogy; the village mourned.

The morning after Ernie's father's funeral, the sun was a clouded orb that shaded the ballfield, casting long shadows that obscured the horizon. From my bed near the window, I could see Ernie sitting alone on the bleachers, holding a Louisville Slugger bat. He had also put on a Tiger baseball uniform, complete with the long socks and cleats worn by the major leaguers. His father had given him this outfit on his last trip home. Ernie wore the familiar Tiger headgear, which he'd bought at the local hardware store. He seemed decked out to play.

He pulled himself up from the bleachers and began walking slowly toward the outfield, dragging his wooden bat behind him. When Ernie reached the right-field fence, he stopped and seemed to look back at my house, almost as if he were sensing my presence. He stood transfixed for a moment with a puzzled expression on his face. Ernie then clambered over the wire fence. When he reached the railroad right of way, he paused and then walked slowly onto the tracks.

Listening and with a sense of dread, I heard the low moan of the train as it circled the bend before it headed in a straight line in the direction of the ballfield. Ernie stared down the track at the oncoming train, eyeing it warily the way a right-handed pitcher faces a left-handed slugger, the bat tucked over his shoulder in readiness. The screech of the wailing whistle and the rush of the air brakes was deafening as the behemoth bore down on him. Sparks of molten metal rained red from the shrieking brakes of the iron wheels, but the train kept hurtling its way toward the fragile boy. Ernie stood his ground.

Frightened that I had only my thoughts to intercede, I stood up from my bed and as quickly as my braces would allow, flung myself over to my window and shouted to the small figure squaring off with the metal monster. I desperately wanted to hold his life in my hands and try by the force of my will to compel him to move. Because of sheer distance, I knew no sound could reach him from me. "Ernie, please!" I hollered, trembling and quaking "Ernie, get off the goddamn tracks."

I thought I could see Ernie look toward my room. He hesitated as the train barreled down on him like an inevitability.

"PLEASE, ERNIE" I shook my fist. "God, let him be."

Though it was impossible, in my mind's eye, I could have sworn I saw him blink. Then Ernie slowly stepped off the track, leaving the bat behind only mere seconds before he would have perished. The train rushed by him with the brakes still screeching like a banshee. The engine caught the bat and blew it into pieces, scattering debris in all directions. As the train screamed by the despairing figure at the side of the tracks, Ernie slumped to his knees, and I thought I could see his shoulders sagging in what I guessed was grief and hopelessness.

I never saw or spoke to Ernie again. The following week his family moved. No one was certain where, but it was speculated that they had moved to another state where Ernie's mother originally hailed from. Perhaps the way our friendship ended was the best that anyone could possibly hope for. I mean, what could either of us have said? I will never know how his life turned out. I suppose I could try to send him a letter, but I wouldn't know where to post it, and more importantly, I wouldn't know what to write.

I spend my retirement years—naturally—watching Tiger baseball on the flatscreen. Ernie Harwell has long since gone to the great ballfield in the sky, but I can still hear his melodious voice in my head. Many times in life there are bitter endings—but after all, I didn't save Ernie's life, he did. The young lad must have wanted life more than death. I can only wonder now if he was pleased with his choice.

After Ernie moved, I asked my parents if I could have a room downstairs. This meant moving into what had been our den, but what the heck, it worked. That summer I began forcing myself to get outside, the metal and leather braces creaking and groaning from this new activity. My father and I learned to play catch together, although maybe a little awkwardly. Every now and then I even hit the ball. I wonder what Ernie Harwell would have said about that?

Looking back, it is perhaps serendipitous that Mr. Harwell was hired by Walter O Briggs Jr., the son of Mr. Briggs Sr. I would truly like to believe that the crumpled letter in Ernie's pocket may have contributed in some minor way to this turn of events.

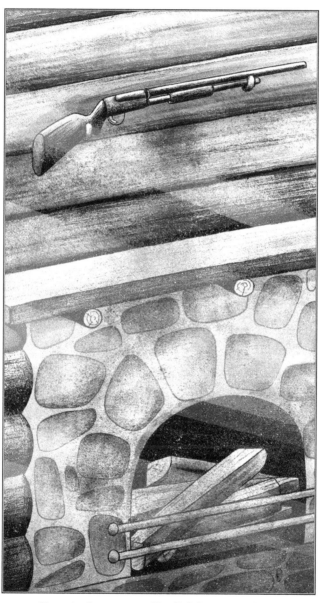

"In my incubus state, a trembling bird clung to a weak limb in the midst of a spring snowstorm."

IV

A Shotgun Wedding

I was just six, but still able to remember my mother screaming at James that I was "demonic, a damn child from hell." I hid quaking under the kitchen table, terrified of her anger and despair.

It is clear to me now, what a cancerous effect my existence must have had on my mother. I never wanted this gift of prophecy and have always considered my abilities an unwanted curse; perhaps even repugnant. As my mother's bouts of depression worsened, I was able to feel her distress, almost palpable, though I was too young to articulate this vicarious pain. Pastor James Martin, Pastor James, to most folks around here, was my stepfather, and he would try to calm my mother's beleaguered mind, but her affliction was too great to be mollified by his gentle touch.

I must preface my history by way of an explanation. While I may have the power of prophecy—I really don't know what else to call it but prophecy—one of the several psychiatrists I sought out over the years called it delusions of grandeur. He inferred that I was enthralled by this very gift and pompously suggested that I wished to bear these unbidden delusions into an exalted existence for all to see. As if, somehow, I needed applause for my pitiful life to be complete. Another high-priced and equally incompetent shrink suggested I indulged in selective memory. I told her I found her allegorical allusion to a pig in mud, and her evaluation that "you seem to be wallowing around in your own mental excrement" disgusting, at which point she promptly fired me as a patient. I made a final plea for help and understanding with my last psychiatrist, a Freudian, suggested that I suffered from an inverted uterus which was responsible for my female hysteria. I gave up—good riddance to all of them.

My earliest recollections are crowded with a series of shadows. Isn't that how all young children perceive their world? A swirl of dark mist that begins to take on shapes of human forms? Or was it just how I came to know the world?

As I was told, it was 1940, the year my parents wed. In Europe, World War II had begun in earnest and the conflict would eventually shatter my parents' quiet existence. At the time my mother; Dolores, was seventeen and quite pregnant. My maternal grandfather insisted that Daniel, Danny for short, my biological father, should marry her. That is where the shadows begin.

It is fair to say that I suppressed many memories. As my late stepfather, James, came close to his impending death, his confessions, which he had withheld for decades, filled in many of the blank spaces of my early life. James died years ago, at a quite advanced age. My mother and biological father are also long gone, so I feel free to write their history. If there was any guilt, legally or morally, for what happened, the truth lies deep in the frigid depths of Lake Baraga, north of Nelson, the remote village closest to this dark expanse of water. I think that lake, whose rock-strewn shore is out my back door, is a fitting tomb for truth, and I see no need to resurrect its full contents, though I do feel compelled to write the story my stepfather shared with me in his later years.

At my birth my mother named me Cassandra, who I later learned from the book Bulfinch's Mythology was the daughter of King Priam and his queen, Hecuba. According to Greek mythology, Cassandra was given the gift of prophecy by Apollo, but when she spurned his advances, he placed a curse upon her. From that moment on, her prophecies, although precise, were never to be believed. I would like to think that my mother picked my name out of erudition or even some small prophetic gift of her own. But the truth seems much simpler: my mother just liked the name. I suppose fate intervened in my life, and like the mythic goddess, I came to believe, whether I liked it or not, that I have a gift for prophecy. Of course, in a world of modern science these options are viewed as silly superstitions. Like the goddess I was absently named for, I was not believed, especially as a child. My parents and other adults put down my prognostications as mere childish daydreaming. So, there you have it, Cassandra—but mother always called me Cassie.

Now, at the turn of the twenty-first century, I am on the cusp of my own death from pancreatic cancer, though, as always, no one believes me, including the goddamn country doc in this backward county. The sad truth is, I'm now considered "a little touched" by many folks around here, though frankly, I don't give a damn.

The village of Nelson lies near the stormy shores of Lake Superior. My biological father was a logger and very familiar with the mean end of a chainsaw. His given name was really Daniel Niemela, but everyone around here just called him Danny. He worked in the woods, and according to locals, drank as hard as he worked. Danny was largely unschooled and rough, and tough as boot nails. I still have a black-and-white photo of him on my mantle, posing with an eight-point swamp buck he had shot. He looks straight at the photographer—my mother; I assume—his eyes penetrating, with almost a ferocity. Did he glimpse his fate? My mother, Dolores, a beautiful lass with long auburn hair, had just graduated from high school, and like many women of that era had no other plans than to marry and have children—but she kind of got those idealized plans out of order. I know from personal experience that passion can be a bane to a young woman, and Danny, at age twenty-one, was all raw energy.

In 1940 an out-of-wedlock pregnancy was an immoral stigma, and my parents were the victims of ugly rumors. Then Mother's condition became very apparent for all to see in this small town. With no other options, she consented to marry Danny.

Daniel made an appointment with the local pastor of the Episcopal church in the town of Bishop just up the road from the village of Nelson. James later in life provided me with an account of the "transaction." Pastor Martin, or James, as I would later learn to call him, was a confirmed, but young, bachelor. He had quietly resisted living in the church parsonage in Bishop, which was in ill repair, and had purchased a small bungalow on Lake Baraga, just north of the village of Nelson.

The pastor had met the couple at the door and welcomed them in. Pastor Martin, who preferred to just be called James greeted Daniel warmly, despite my father's religious ignorance. Dolores's family were steady Episcopalians and attended his church, while Daniel, he only knew by reputation. Nelson was a small village, after all. The couple perched nervously on the edge of a threadbare couch in the informal parsonage; Danny coughed, while Dolores twisted a handkerchief in her hands.

The pastor, a tall young man with a pleasant smile, sat silently waiting for Danny to speak.

"I know I don't go to your church," Danny finally said. "In fact, I don't go to no church, but the fact is we need to get married."

The pastor regarded Daniel. The young man had emphasized the word, "need," and James could tell from the young girl's protruding belly that yes, it was a case of need.

The minister cleared his throat. "Generally, I perform marital counseling for several months before I agree to marry a couple."

"We ain't got months," Danny said gruffly.

"Hmm, yes, I can see that."

Dolores blushed.

"We'd go to the magistrate, but her father told me we gotta' get married in the church," Danny said bluntly. "Will you marry us or not?"

The pastor studied the young woman, struck by her pleasing countenance, which he thought harkened back to the Renaissance age, or perhaps even the age of antiquity. Though well-schooled in theology, he had always been appreciative of intrinsic beauty and had collected a series of fanciful nude female images that he kept secretly locked away in his bedroom end table. Sighing, he prepared himself for the inevitable question he had to ask.

"Before I answer that, Daniel, let me ask you

something, Dolores." He hesitated, meeting her entrancing green eyes. "Dolores, if you weren't in a family way, would you want to marry Daniel?"

She looked aghast, as if she had never considered this question. "Well, I mean, I suppose so," she said testily. "I mean, what choice do I have?" Her eyes flared with anger. "I can't raise a bastard here in this community. The child would be the laughing stock of the town."

Danny twisted on the couch like a worm impaled on a hook. "You know, Dolores, you don't gotta' marry me. Other women in this town think I would be a good catch."

"You mean that slut Sherilyn?" she spit out. "She's slept with half the men in town. Who in the hell would want to marry her? Why she—"

"I think I should withdraw my question," Pastor Martin interrupted. "It is clear that Dolores needs a father for her child and maybe that's reason enough for me to marry the two of you. Perhaps we should set a date for the nuptials."

Danny straightened. "There is one more question I'd like to know before we go through with this—what do you plan on charging to marry us, cuzz I don't have much money left after rent and my truck payment."

The pastor knew a skinflint when he saw one, "How about twenty dollars?"

Danny seemed to gnaw on this proposal. "Tell you what, I ain't got much money but I've got a nice twenty-gauge shotgun, bolt action, with a three-shell clip I'll trade for the wedding ceremony. Believe me, you would be getting the better end of the deal."

Apparently, Dolores was to be bargained off like a piece of second-hand furniture. Dolores had grimaced silently at Danny's proposal, but to Pastor Martin her eyes spoke eloquently.

The minister nodded, and they shook hands on the deal. I guess you could call this ironic arrangement a shotgun wedding and leave it at that, but that wasn't the end of the story.

I was born in the Bishop Memorial Hospital on December 22, 1940. I won't say my birth was uneventful; only an ignorant man would say that. Deliveries are always a painful affair, fraught with the possibility of problems. As it was, I was born with ten fingers and ten toes, which at that time was a medical indicator of a normal birth.

The village of Nelson hugs the inland rock-strewn shores of Lake Baraga, a lake highly recommended by local fishermen. A mix of hardwood and conifers grip its shore like an iron vise of sorts, with enormous boulders that clamp the ragged edge of the lake and to this day remain a barrier to development. After the wedding Daniel and Dolores moved into a sparse cabin on the lake that Father bought from Charlie Swanson's widow, Elizabeth, after she got tired of living in the sticks and wanted to move to Nelson. Charlie had died years before from ethanol poisoning, but Lizzie, as she was called, had clung on there alone for better than two decades. Elizabeth had lived in the rustic cabin for years and never felt the need to fix the place up. I don't think Father paid much for the shack but it was all he could afford at the time with his meager savings. It is prime real estate now but at the time was little more than a crude hovel.

The bitter cold would suck through the rough-cut trim of the old casements, leaving winter's snow deposited on the windowsills like congealed pudding. Mother would stuff all our rag rugs against the bottom of the drafty doors to stop the icy wind from entering this miserable excuse for a house. I don't remember much of the first four years of my life; who does? I suppose my parents got along all right, despite the mean living my father provided as a sawyer. Maybe, if the war hadn't intruded into their lives, this story might have turned out differently; but the war changed everything.

Toward the end of the hostilities, my father was drafted. My mother later told James that I had predicted his departure in childish chatter. I assume this story was accurate but have no recollection of this event. At the time Mother was just amused by my childish premonitions—but this would later change.

After basic training, Father was to report to Fort Bragg, North Carolina, for active duty. He was assigned to the motor pool and came home for the usual leave before catching the Greyhound bus back to Fort Bragg. I have some memories of that time, like the shadows

I mentioned earlier. I remember them arguing but what about, I have no idea. Perhaps sex or money; isn't that what most couples argue about?

When my father's leave was up, I recall staring out the window as he walked to the gas station, where he was to meet the bus for his return to base. Mother stood beside me.

Tears dripped down my face. "Daddy die, Daddy die."

"No," my mother said. "I know you don't understand this, Cassie, but he won't die. He is in the motor pool, a long way from the front lines. It will be all right. Don't worry." Though only five I recall my hurt that my mother had minimized my vision. To my mother it was as if I had spouted a silly childhood comment, all nonsense, or worse yet gibberish. But even at that age, I knew what I knew.

A year passed, which I have little memory of, however in the following January or early February, despite the harsh winter, the sun appeared bright in the sky, as if a rebuke to the frigid weather. Looking out the window, I wondered why there were snowshoe tracks on the lake that seemed to be coming and going from our house. I was six.

"Momma, look, tracks," I said, pointing out the window.

"Yes, an ice fisherman I guess, Cassie."

"No, Momma, come see. The tracks come to the house," I said "Man come see you."

"You're mistaken, Cassie," she said emphatically, looking away.

I remember feeling puzzled. I waited at the front window most of the day, watching for the ice fisherman to come into view. No one appeared. By evening the snowshoe tracks had folded into white crusts and disappeared. The sun was bright on the frozen lake the following morning, and new fresh snow covered the expanse. The snowshoe tracks reappeared. There were several fishermen on the ice that morning, so my childhood curiosity was satisfied and I sought other diversions. In the following days I accepted the frequently occurring tracks coming to and from our house as nothing out of the ordinary.

It wasn't long afterward, though, that I chatted to my mother, "Momma, you have a baby."

She stared at me in astonishment. "Of course not," she stammered, "that couldn't happen. Where did you get such an idea, Cassie?"

"The wind tell me."

"Don't be silly, Cassie. The wind doesn't talk."

"It talk to me. It tell me everything, Momma."

Shortly thereafter, my mother wrote my father asking for a divorce. I remember being sleepily bundled into James' old Buick and waking up on a chilly morning in a strange house on the other side of the lake. I was confused but mother quietly explained to me that Pastor Martin was going to be my new father.

Pastor Martin bent down and took my hand in his.

"I know this is all new, but I think we will get along fine together. If you want you can just call me James," which I did, not understanding this new relationship. It wasn't until I was an adult that James told me that the next day, he had resigned from his charge as the priest of the Episcopalian church in Bishop. I suppose that was honorable, or maybe the word isn't honorable, but convenient, as Mother was already noticeably pregnant with his child.

It was in the early stages of spring, and the winter was shedding her fury; ice lay thin on the lake; the ground was still frozen. Smoke curled upward from our former dwelling on the far side of the lake. I thought that the remaining ice reminded me of my mother's meringue pies.

"Daddy come home," I predicted cheerfully, much to mother's and James's dismay.

"I doubt it, Cassie," James said nervously.

Daniel, having completed his Army duties got rip-roaring drunk and kicked in the door late that evening, cursing and shouting at Dolores and James. "Get up, you fucking whore," he yelled at my mother. "You will pay for leavin' me, you goddamn slut."

The nightmare of the World War might have ended, but my father's rage was ignited like an unquenchable fire. He stormed through James' house, busting furniture and lamps and yelling profanities at the cowering pair.

"You think, Dolores, that I'm just gonna' give up

on our marriage and let you steal Cassie?" he shouted. "Cuzz I ain't, You gotta' have reasons for divorce in this state, damnit."

James straightened, and in my mind cast a shadow over Danny. "How about irreconcilable differences, Danny? And if that isn't enough, a certain female named Sherilyn told me in confession that she slept with you after you were married to Dolores. The law calls that adultery and grounds for divorce."

Danny sucked in a breath, dumbfounded. "You can't use what was said in a confessional against me. That's unethical and probably would end your damn career."

James' voice grew quiet. "This may come as a surprise to you, but I quit the Episcopal church when Dolores moved in with me, so I can tell the judge anything I want. You won't be able to stop what is inevitable. There will be a divorce, and Dolores will get custody of Cassie. If you care about ever seeing your child again, you will go along with this divorce."

Danny stood still, stunned perhaps like a wounded animal, and for a time apparently unsure how to react. He sank to his knees, the lamp that he held still in his hand. He bowed his head as if in prayer, then looked upward as if he understood that there was no changing this terrible twist of fate that had been imposed on him, not only by circumstances, but perhaps by a design that he couldn't quite fathom.

"Well, Pastor, seems like I'm the fucking loser," he

said, finally sobbing quietly. "I won't stand in your way."

I couldn't understand what was happening, just that my world was changing. Daniel lifted me up, a solitary tear trickling down his face. He planted a kiss on my forehead and set me down again.

"Don't go...Daddy die."

I remember Daniel looked perplexed, and he stared at me as if trying to frame a question.

"There is just one more thing, Pastor. I want my shotgun back. It's the least you can do since you broke the goddamn deal. It was a gift from my old man, and I have sentimental feelings toward the thing."

James hesitated, but knowing there wasn't any ammunition in the shotgun or, for that matter, in the house, he took what he thought was just a wall-hanger down off the wall and handed it to my father. Daniel opened the breech, pulled three shells from the wool pocket of his coat, and deftly loaded the clip of the old piece.

James gaped incredulously at him. "What do you intend to do now, Danny? If you think that harming us will make the world right, I guess I have misread you."

Danny pointed the shotgun at James. "Bang," he said, laughing menacingly. Then turning, he aimed the shotgun at Dolores. "Bang," he said again, all the while laughing in a maniacal manner. Drunk and unsteady, he stumbled out of the house and onto the treacherous ice. He shifted back and forth in the strengthening wind, as snow squalls obscured the deepening half-light.

The precarious frozen lake lay in front of him. Danny stepped onto the dangerously unstable sheet of ice left over from the spring melt.

James and my mother watched in the dimming end of daylight as he wove, unsure of his dangerous path across the thin ice of Lake Baraga toward his house—and my previous home. Midpoint in the lake, Father seemed to stare over his shoulder at us as he shed his plaid hunting coat and laid it haphazardly on the ice. James' and Delores' expressions turned to utter horror as my father shot the ice around his feet in three rapid shots, emptying the clip. The percussion and dreadful impact of the charges cracked the fragile ice, and his hulking frame sank out of sight. I remember Delores weeping almost inconsolably as James tried to comfort her. Later, I was left alone in my bedroom and cried myself to sleep.

Several days later the deputy sheriff showed up at our door, wondering if James and Delores knew of Danny's whereabouts, as he had been reported missing. James related to the deputy that they had no idea where he was while Mother, despite her hidden grief, sarcastically added that the deputy should check all the bars in the area, as that was the most likely place to find him. The following day Danny's plaid hunting coat and the large jagged hole through the rotten ice was discovered by an ice fisherman, who reported it to the authorities.

At this point the sheriff's department assumed

Danny had fallen through the ice and drowned. The sheriff later informed our small-town newspaper that there were no witnesses to my father's fall through the ice. The investigation was put on hold till spring, after the ice was gone. I once overheard James and Dolores whispering that they must have been the only ones who had heard the three eerie shots from the old shotgun, I can only assume now that they never had any intention of telling the sheriff what they knew.

The shotgun was never found, and my best guess is that the old weapon still lies on the muddy bottom of Lake Baraga. My father's remains were found in mid-spring, after the sheriff had dutifully dragged the lake. No shotgun holes were found in the corpse, so consequently my father's death was ruled an accidental drowning by the aging coroner. My mother cried in ever-deepening bouts of grief, remembering my omen of his demise. "You knew, Cassie. You knew."

I remember awakening afraid and almost convulsing from a vision later that spring. In my incubus state, a trembling bird clung precariously to a weak limb in the midst of a spring snowstorm. I vividly recall that the bird, which seemed to be almost feminine and ethereal in some sense—perhaps a mourning dove—yet not, had fallen lifeless to the ground, the frigid twisting wind covered the dead form in a shifting white snowdrift. I tried to tell James about my vision, screaming that my mother was going to die. He dismissed it as a nightmare and told me that everything would be all right. I distinctly remember that he kissed me on the forehead and told me to go back to sleep.

James and Dolores married at the courthouse shortly after Daniel was legally given up for dead.

I have little recall of the next several months, but later in life James told me that my mother fell into a deep depression, so debilitating that hospitalization in Marquette, a larger city, was required. Crude and ineffective depression medications were tried on her without success. I was to believe later that my inability to remember any of this was as much a product of the self-protective nature of my gift as it was my psychiatrist's notion that I had suppressed this traumatic event.

"I am at fault for Danny's death," Mother wailed in despair to James; and later, "Our affair killed him." I have no formal training in the workings of the mind but it seems clear that my mother was besieged by guilt so severe that she was emotionally crippled.

Her psychiatrist used the primitive electric convulsion therapy on my mother, but without any clinical success. James felt the medical use of deliberate convulsions was almost a criminal act, but the doctors argued otherwise, and so he conceded to what he thought was a barbaric administration of medical torture. At the time no anesthetics or muscle relaxants were used, so the process could be quite painful. James watched in horror as his wife writhed in pain. Unfortunately, she only got worse and was finally discharged, a broken woman.

Shortly after Christmas, December 27, 1946, my

mother, still pregnant with James' child, put her head in the oven and turned on the gas fulfilling my dreaded augury. I would like to say she died peacefully, but no, I think she was tortured, at least in her own mind. Regrets can be as poisonous as bottled gas and just as deadly.

Now as a reluctant oracle, I choose to remain mostly silent in the face of future omens, as nobody ever believed me anyway. I am reminded of a sermon that James preached one Easter Sunday. He spoke of the denial of Jesus' spoken truth about the coming kingdom of God, and how Christ had not been accepted by the majority of Gentiles and Jews alike. During that Easter service he solemnly quoted a King James scripture, Luke chapter 4:24. And Jesus spoke, "verily I say unto you. No prophet is accepted in his own land." Truer words have never been spoken.

I believe that most humans would rather believe in some dark mythical sense of fate rather than a divinely inspired premonition. Cassandras since the age of antiquity have been largely ignored by one and all; I am no exception.

After my mother's death, James re-entered the ministry and transferred to Methodism, where he pastored the rest of his life in the village of Nelson. James later remarried and had four boys in the process, none of whom I am close to, except perhaps Robert, who is incarcerated and to whom I write on occasion. Despite what might have been his silent misgivings, James legally adopted me and lovingly raised me as his own. He died tortured by guilt, I suppose, at the age of eighty-three. James never told his sons of the origin of his flawed relationship to my mother or the subsequent suicide of my father; or for that matter, the lie that he and my mother so closely kept secreted away from the world. To the best of my knowledge only his son Robert has any inkling of the cause of his father's plunge into mental illness at the end of his life. I believe the lies he harbored tormented him late in life and were probably the cause of his dreadful unhinging, rather than the tragic suicide of either Daniel or Delores.

I must pass on one more revelation of my life. Several years ago, a carpenter, while tearing up my old floorboards in my house—the same house on Lake Baraga, by the way, that James had willed to me—discovered a box of old letters hidden underneath the bedroom floor. I assume the letters were hidden by my mother, but who knows, perhaps James. I have read, and reread the letters from my deceased father Daniel many times. The evocative letters written to me, his young daughter Cassie, were almost mind-numbing and left me in tears. The letters, now yellowed with age, were postmarked toward the end of the war. For the most part, they offered mundane accounts of his life in the army. But in later letters the events turned dark as he recounted a Japanese attack on his motor pool in the Philippines after he had been stationed near the front lines. That was the last letter written by his own hand. One poignant letter tucked into the others, however, was heart-sickening. In that last postmarked letter, a Red Cross volunteer recounted that tragic attack and reported that Daniel had suffered a severe shrapnel wound to his head. This disclosure was difficult for me to accept, as James had never spoken of my father's injuries, or for that matter these letters, I would expect that my mother must have been emotionally distraught by my father's injuries and that in some ways his wounds affected her own fragile mental state. The letter details his difficult and incomplete recovery in a stateside hospital, and finally explained that he suffered from both physical and mental trauma, evidently due to the effects of both war and distress from home. He was discharged from the Army as unfit for active duty. End of story.

A postscript: I, like my mother, became pregnant at an early age. I birthed a daughter I christened Milcah, and later a son whom I named Edward. I, most assuredly, did not name my daughter Cassandra.

When the mood strikes me, I put on my floppy purple hat and sunglasses and play the slots at the local Indian Casino in Marquette. I often win; of course, the casino doesn't know that with my gift I have a decided advantage. My new shrink, a true cynic, calls it dumb luck. Regardless, I keep my winnings small so I don't attract unnecessary attention.

As for me, I am called Cassie the Cat Lady around Nelson; thirty-seven felines at last count—but maybe more, don't know. When I pass, the administrator of my estate has been directed to place a headstone upon my biological father's place of burial. Currently, and perhaps unjustly, Daniel's gravesite is marked with only a solitary wooden cross, which understandably has deteriorated with age. I have legally arranged that my mother's cremated remains be moved from their present resting place next to James, and be reinterred next to Daniel's gravesite. Additionally, I directed that their headstone be inscribed as follows: "Here lies Daniel Niemela and Dolores Niemela, husband and wife. May they rest in peace." I have also requested that my ashes be interred in the gravesite next to theirs. Perhaps there is no fairness in the matter of death, but I have personally determined to make proper amends as least as much as humanly possible, for the ugly hands of fate. In truth, I really don't think James would mind. He was a very gracious man and I truly miss him.

I know my end is coming—sooner rather than later—and it is my last wish that my beloved cats inherit my house and the adequate trust fund that I have established for their care and upkeep. As for my daughter Milcah, well she will carry on I suppose, with or without my dear son Edward. That is another story.

I can't help but laugh, but one sultry summer day last year Sheriff Morley stopped by and made veiled threats about animal cruelty and nuisance laws. I informed him that my cats are treated better than the inmates in his lockup. He just shrugged his shoulders without commenting. When he went into my place to inspect my home for health and safety reasons—without a warrant, I might add—I surreptitiously slipped a bag of ripe cat shit into the back seat of his patrol car. Perhaps truly the best way to let the cat out of the bag.

"I do not think, as much as I dwell, on the past."

V

A Dog Named Bunny

"Get your goddamn dog out of my garden! He just shat in my pea patch," old lady Larsen hollered. I shouted at Bunny, our mutt, and she came running as if her ass was on fire. She knew when to get the hell outta' the neighbor lady's garden—but I always thought the darn dog didn't give a damn. If a dog can have a nemesis, old lady Larsen was surely Bunny's.

I flinch inwardly. My first lines that I write are some of the most painful to express.

I lay my pen down and roll over on my bunk. I am incarcerated in a minimum-security prison: Marquette Branch, in the heart of the Upper Peninsula of Michigan. I am aware that there is no escaping, either my past or this wretched prison cell. To physically escape from this joint, I would have to climb over a tall fence ringed with savage concertina wire that would rip a man to shreds, and even if one could broach the wire, the endless swamps teaming with relentless clouds of blackflies and hordes of ravenous mosquitoes would drive a man crazy long before he found himself a safe refuge. Likewise, in winter, the freezing cold and deep snow would prove just as formidable, as one could find no quarter anywhere from the harsh elements of the Upper Peninsula. Believe me, I have considered all the possibilities, and come to the conclusion that I will rot here like an overripened fruit.

Memories are sometimes the only thing I have to engage my attention—I do not think, as much as I dwell, on the past. It's lights out time. Low murmurs and quiet whisperings rise from the cell block as if a bizarre form of a church service. I have borrowed a thesaurus from the library and intend to use it. Some slivers of pallid moonlight filter in through the heavily barred windows, enough to write. I pause and jot down another line, aware that likely the only reader of this assigned memoir will be you, the overworked English teacher here in lockup. You have given our small, motley group of inmates an assignment: write a memoir, which I will make an effort to pen despite my confusion on what is required. I suppose what you want is a collection of stories, or maybe not. Don't really know. I find this class assignment difficult in some ways, given I only finished the eighth grade before I got sent up. You tell me I am intellectually much further on than my formal eighth grade education would indicate; I don't know, but I do read a lot, damn little else to do here. Of course, my job in the prison library could be a factor too; books are like magnets to me.

I continue; where to start? It is reasonable to wonder how our family came to name their new pup, a Christmas gift in 1964, after a rabbit, but there you have it—Bunny. I suppose I could blame my lack of recall on my tender age, but I can't. As the old saying goes, "A lot of water has gone under the bridge." I suppose I should give you the family rundown so all that happened might be clearer; according to you the proper term for this review is called backstory. Anyway, my older half-sister, Cassie, was twenty-four and dropped out of college during my lengthy trial. My twin brother Duane and I (Robert) were fifteen, and truly typical teenagers. My younger brother Alan was seven, while William (Bill) was four, and the youngest, Hank, was just a baby at that time. All of us boys were products of my father's second marriage to Lena, our dear and devout mother who died tragically giving birth to Hank. I will try not to give you too much boring personal history but feel the need to fill in the blank spaces on my notepad. Maybe all of that makes for poor form in a memoir but there you have it. My father, Pastor James Martin, adopted Cassie after his first wife, Delores, pregnant, committed suicide—stuck her head in a damn oven from what Cassie once told me. Lena was the attractive church organist, and married at the time to a local contractor, but I guess that didn't stop my old man from getting involved with her. Despite being a minister, my father always had an eye for well-built women, which my mother was; on several occasions this penchant, (word I found in the thesaurus) got him in trouble with the church hierarchy.

But all of that will have to come later and isn't relevant to the story you requested us to write. I'm twenty-four now. The point is I don't remember how Bunny got her name so the best I can do is guess. The pup, part collie and part beagle, had fluffy white ears and short stature; not sure a dog has stature, but hope you get the point. She was built close to the ground, so in our young eyes we might have seen the whelp as "bunny-like." Regrettably, because the old man is gone and given that I am locked up, I rarely communicate with my brothers, so I can't inquire of the only other humans who might have a clue. Anyway, the origin of the name isn't the point of my tale; but my father's losses and his painful lie are—though strictly speaking it was to the best of my knowledge the only lie he ever told me; although Cassie has hinted otherwise.

My father was a man of meager means. Fact is, most pastors are poor. A tall and lean parson, Pastor James Martin had a rural charge in the village of Nelson in the Upper Peninsula of Michigan. Nelson is just a dot on the map of the Upper Peninsula, a village in name only, a few houses, general store, gas station, Dad's church, three room school, and such, surrounded by miles upon miles of near wilderness. Everywhere you look around Nelson you see trees, like a veritable ocean of green when the leaves are out, and so many pure lakes and trout streams hiding in the shadows of the Huron Mountains that I never tired of fishing a new one with the old man. I guess it is fair to say, it was like a young man's heaven on earth.

Father was in his middle years when he married our younger mother, Lena. As I mentioned, she passed while giving birth to Hank. She hemorrhaged, leaving my despondent father with five young boys to raise. I suppose with a pup, he hoped to make up for her loss the previous year. It was a noble gesture, as they say, but the loss of a mother is such a severe psychological blow that the impact often pummels a child for an entire life. The death of a parent is not a unique event; I just mention it to frame the picture of my life and not for pity. I suppose I could just say she was dead and leave it at that, but my father's need to compensate his boys for her untimely death remains a tragic but endearing feature of his difficult life, and the very source of this tragic story.

I was fifteen when we opened the Christmas box, where the pup was sleeping. The pup shook off her sleep, slowly opening her eyes, as if trying to make sense out of this new world she found before her. My younger brothers giggled with delight as the pup tipped over the box and scampered around, growling and yipping with fervor and knocking ornaments off the tree. She managed to bust a couple of ornaments, which should have been a prophetic sign of what was to come.

As a pup Bunny was our constant companion. The first few weeks were both a pleasure and much effort. She loved to chew and made my father angry when she attacked his lambskin slippers with a sense of abandon that could only be likened to Attila the Hun's sack of Rome. She also shredded the corner of a footstool and savaged the leg of Dad's favorite antique rocker; that, and her being stubborn about not wanting to go outside to do her business, dampened my father's enthusiasm for Bunny. My brothers and I cleaned up after Bunny and tried to mollify (another word from the thesaurus) father, but sometimes we weren't successful. After the attack on Dad's rocker, us boys got together and bought a steak from the general store and grilled it as a surprise for him. We set the sizzling steak in front of Dad and watched in horror as Bunny leapt up on the kitchen chair and snatched it off Dad's plate and scrambled away with it. We tried to run Bunny down but she sucked the steak down like it was a stick of hot butter. Father, pissed and swearing, threw his steak knife at Bunny just missing the fleeing mutt. Believe me, this was not as funny at the time, as it seems now.

As the pup grew in the following year my younger brothers would wrestle and scramble about in the yard, Bunny yapping and barking and causing all kinds of ruckus, till the old lady next door would finally tire of it and pound on the parsonage door, yelling at my father to "Shush the damn noise." I suppose the old biddy thought we were a bunch of heathens, even though our father was the lone preacher in the rural village. According to local gossip, Mrs. Larsen's late husband had died shortly after their wedding decades before. My father had once quipped that her husband probably preferred death and damnation over living with that nasty bitch. Despite being a preacher, at times Father could be quite caustic.

My brothers and I knew Dad's personal side, which he rarely publicly displayed. He would swear and cuss when us boys got out of hand, and we also know he kept a bottle of Jack Daniels and a few Playboy magazines tucked away in his desk drawer. His demeanor reminded me of a chameleon in that he could blend into his surroundings and purposely not be notable. My best guess is that most effective pastors are similar to the chameleon—infrequently displaying their true colors. It probably has much to do with self-preservation. Even as a young man it was my observation that most parishioners didn't care for outspoken ministers, preferring known quantities of tepid milquetoast instead.

I should mention one more thing about old lady Larsen: she raised chickens in an outdoor coop behind her ramshackle home. Mrs. Larsen was a bone-slender, hard-faced woman with noticeable scoliosis. She seemed content to wear baggy hand-me-down men's trousers with an overly long belt and on her head she sported a bedraggled black fedora. After many complaints by neighbors, she had fenced in her yard and garden with chicken wire to keep out the varmints and to eliminate the inevitable chicken shit deposited on the nearby ballfield where all us boys hung out. On overly warm days the smell of fresh chicken shit hung in the air. Remembering back on it, the fetid stench seemed almost sulfurous, eliciting visions of a surrealistic xanthous storm cloud hanging over the village; later I would call this another portent.

Bunny proved to be an easy train, picking up the usual tricks: she sat, would lie down, beg, come when called; you know, all those various tricks that humans think are necessary, and to my best guess, dogs believe are stupid.

I don't mean to imply that Bunny was a model of a perfect pet; she had her faults. She would dig holes randomly all over our dandelion-infested yard, till the lawn looked like it had been used by the Army for mortar practice. This canine habit made it necessary to fill the damn holes every time my father forced me to mow the yard. Of course, as soon as I finished mowing, Bunny, as if offended by my labor, would start digging again. This was a war that lasted her entire life.

Another one of her apparent faults was her antipathy for Joey, the fat paperboy, who would come tearing down the sidewalk on his red Schwinn bike and just heave the newspaper into the yard, a logical maneuver to avoid Bunny's consistent charge. She would chase him the length of the lot, snapping and growling, and lunging at his pant leg. I thought this was quite fun to watch, and unbeknownst to my father, would deliberately let Bunny out of our house when I saw Joey coming our way. I would laugh uproariously at this daily event, which I surreptitiously spied on through the parsonage window. Joey would pedal like some kind of wailing banshee, yelling and kicking at Bunny's onslaught, and never figured out that I was the instigator.

I've heard another cliché that "All good things must come to an end," and this amusing trounce finally came to an abrupt halt when Bunny finally got a hold of one of Joey's pant legs and pulled him down in a pile of boy, bike, and snarling dog, going ass-end-over-teakettle on the unyielding concrete sidewalk. Bunny refused to give up her pant leg, and Joey, knees and elbows skinned and bleeding, finally extracted himself by unbuckling his pants and sliding out of them. At first Bunny looked quizzical, as if she might let up on the poor young buck, but in a show of defiance, she grabbed hold of his patterned boxers and with one savage rip, the boxers shredded, leaving Joey running down the street butt naked.

Hearing all the commotion, my father came running, fearing a tragedy of some sort. He saw the final act and me laughing hysterically. Needless to say, he was not amused, and I was grounded for a week. While I disliked the punishment, I still think I got the better end of the deal. My father caught another round of verbal abuse that evening, but this time it was from Joey's dad, a former Army drill sergeant who cussed my father out in what I would call very colorful language. Dad unhappily ponied up, paying for new boxers and a pair of trousers. After that incident, Dad made a rule that Bunny had to be inside between four and four-thirty, when Joey made his appointed rounds. I knew better than to not follow a direct order. Although on Bunny's part, she never barked out the window or strained to mangle Joey again. Perhaps having caught him once, the game was over with the dog convinced that she had nothing left to prove.

While my father had his share of almost comedic disasters with Bunny, he had many delightful days hunting grouse in the maple leaf fall, when trees in the local hardwood forests dripped color laden leaves like so much honey. On occasion, he let me ride along, and we would hunt together, of which I still have fond memories. We would stop at likely young poplar stands and let Bunny out to do her work. Though she didn't look like any bird dog I'd ever seen, she probably would have taken that observation as an insult. She helped my father and me get in close to a grouse and waited till the old man told her to flush—and flush she did. She'd rush in with so much enthusiasm that one time she ran over the damn bird, sending it head over tail till it got its frightened equilibrium back in order, then the bird burst skyward. Dad shot it, a clean hit. He smiled and gave Bunny a well-deserved treat.

"You're one damn good dog," he said, beaming. "What do you think, Robert?"

I nodded, impressed by my father's acumen in his choice of a dog.

I remember Dad and I were once walking a two-track, Dad carrying his old double-barrel shotgun and me a youth model 410. The rutted trail was way back off the Baraga Plains. A late model pickup, with not a scratch on it, pulled up, and the owner leaned out the window. A fine-looking English Pointer stuck its nose out, and if I hadn't known better, fixed his gaze haughtily on Bunny.

The well-dressed hunter frowned as if bemused.

"What kind of bird dog do you call it?" he said sarcastically, with an emphasis on the word "it."

Father just gazed back, straight-faced. "She is an AKC Fiffer Flusher."

"A what?"

"A Fiffer Flusher."

At this point, I wondered if this city dweller might guess that he was being put on. "Well, does your Fiffer Flusher hunt?" He gloated, holding up two grouse.

My father took off his hunting vest and dipped into the deep pocket. "Let's see." He pulled out two grouse and held them aloft. He looked back in the vest. "Oh, my gosh, I guess there is one more here. That makes three. So, by my count my two-dollar dog out-hunted your precious pedigreed pooch." Dad smiled politely. Without uttering another word, the cowed hunter rolled up his window and bounced along the rutted trail and out of sight.

Teach, I have often thought that life spins in concentric circles as if winding tighter, contracting—or at other times in my life, almost antithetically, (thesaurus) the rings seemed to expand outwards. Reminds me of a Swiss watch-spring. Maybe the whole process depends on the whims of some unknown force. Some people call this process the will of God; some don't. As I look back, the circle that Bunny gave our family was tightening, like the watch spring overtwisted by the hands of fate, or by the hands of God; you can draw your own conclusions.

It was in the spring when Bunny took a liking for old lady Larsen's chickens. I should mention that Mrs. Larsen didn't like me at all. She once caught me antagonizing her hens by chucking rocks at them—which I admit I did—causing the chickens to run around squawking and raising a ruckus. As most anyone who has ever raised chickens knows, a riled chicken won't lay eggs, and Mrs. Larsen blamed the lack of eggs that week on me—which was probably accurate. On the other hand, she seemed to adore my younger brother Alan, who she thought could do no wrong. The old hag was always giving him treats from her kitchen. Later, her attachment to Alan was to cause an unintentional series of disastrous events that deeply haunts me still.

One day in early June, Bunny had evidently dug a hole under the fence, and as the old lady watched in horror out her kitchen window, tossed chickens around in the air like an erratic ride at a small-town carnival. Miss Larsen chased Bunny out of her yard with a broom, but not before Bunny had killed several of the old lady's prize hens. Speaking of chickens, as the old cliché goes, she was mad as a wet hen. She stomped angrily over to the parsonage and chewed out my old man, demanding we "shoot the damn dog."

By this time Bunny sat nonchalantly on the front porch, chewing on chicken feathers, her mouth covered with fresh, red chicken blood. My father, unhappily aroused from his nap, used his most calm pastoral voice to quell the old lady's anger.

"I'm very sorry, Mrs. Larsen. I will be happy to pay a fair price for the chickens. What do you think is fair?"

"I don't want your money. I want you to shoot that damn dog!" Her voice was like steel.

Dad wasn't above playing the sympathy card. "You know this dog means so much to the boys, especially since the death of their mother."

My father's conciliatory tone and his judicious use of any pity she might have felt deflated her anger like a party balloon late in the day.

I could see her visibly suck in a breath. "Well, the Leghorns are good layers, and as you know, I sell eggs to get by. So—I will probably lose at least six dozen eggs till the next bantams get laying size. I think six dollars is fair for the eggs." She paused. "But there is the chicken meat to consider—"

My father winced.

"To be fair, the layers only are good for stewing, but since the damn dog killed three, I think they're worth a buck a piece, so that makes a total of nine dollars," she calculated.

Dad opened his well-worn wallet and handed her the nine dollars, which we could ill afford to lose. It wasn't lost on my father that although she was going to charge him for the dead chickens, the layers were probably going to end the day in her stewpot and she hadn't offered to give us any of the future stew.

"If this ever happens again, I'm calling the sheriff," she said, barely mollified. "I suggest you keep your chicken killer chained up."

Which in all honesty we tried, but the moment we chained up Bunny, she would howl and yip and make such a commotion that several other neighbors complained about the noise. In the end we brought her inside, which was an imperfect solution for both man and beast.

Of course, the inevitable happened. My brother Alan left the back door open, and Bunny scrambled out and made a beeline under the fence and to the chicken coop. This time Bunny killed four more chickens, and true to her threat, old lady Larsen called the sheriff.

Later that same day, there came the promised but dreadful knock on the door. Dad was expecting the sheriff, whom he knew from their passing acquaintance in the local Rotary Club in the town of Bishop up the way.

"Hello, Pastor," the hulking deputy sheriff said pleasantly. "Sorry to bother you, but your neighbor lady tells me that your dog has killed some of her chickens."

"Yes, I'm sorry to say, that's true."

"Hmm," the sheriff said. "Seems we got a problem. I—"

"Sheriff, can you wait a moment?" Dad interrupted. He nodded.

"Boys, please go up to your rooms." We hesitated, wanting to know Bunny's fate. "Now," he said sternly.

My father later told us that he thought the best place for Bunny was with a local farmer, and he would find him a home. The younger boys cried at this prospect, but we knew there was no sense in arguing with his decision.

Hey, Teach: Just a note. I admit that this assignment stumps me. I'm not sure I quite know exactly what you want, but I will carry on. The prison library is inadequate in many respects, but sometimes you can find a great read. I have been soaking up Michener's Chesapeake and was enthralled by his vivid sense of person and the scope of history. I know you have told the class that the use of clichés shows a lack of originality, but I think otherwise. To my way of thinking a well-executed cliché is the "poetry of the poorly educated," not much different than poems by Lord Byron or Wallace Stevens are to the well-educated, which I admit I only know by chance after I found a dogeared copy of a poetry book in the library. Indeed, most of us under-educated prisoners are blessed by the inherent poetry of clichés. I am reminded of another cliché that I stole from a soap opera on television, and that is "Time slips by like sand in an hourglass." Time isn't precious here in lockup. We got too damn much, so I rip through a couple of books a week. I think that the whole notion of time is more like the estuary that Michener described, where during the span between the ebb and flood tides, the current seems to stand still—fixed and unmoving. This seems noteworthy to me—that a river, like time, may be neither moving nor unmoving, but elements of both at the same time. I think my father's time on earth, was much like the estuary. While his life moved on, it was not without painful determination, and his time, like the estuary, was a mix of salt marsh and freshwater turned brackish and turbid, dark with suspended foul matter. I doubt he could have changed the outcome, which seems inevitable now. I would have wished differently for him, and ultimately for myself as well, but our losses were too significant.

As my father aged and his health declined, he visited me less and less often. He blamed his health as the reason, but I knew the pain of seeing me incarcerated was often more than he could bear. On a cold December visit, late in his life, he told me he had something he needed to get off his chest. He breathed slowly, with great exertion. An unsmiling prison guard stood in the background, a constant reminder that privacy was not an option.

"Robert," he whispered hoarsely, he never called me Robbie, "I have a confession to make, one that I should have made long ago."

"What is it, Dad?"

"I lied to you boys once—about Bunny," he murmured.

"Everyone has told a lie at some point or the other, Father," I said, acutely aware of my own failures.

"That may be so, but the sin occurs when you don't confess the act," he said, pausing to wheeze. "And I believe that expiation only comes from heartfelt contrition."

"I'm not sure I understand, Dad."

"Yes, perhaps I am being too theological." He smiled and then coughed. "All this has to do with your dog." He sighed. "Yes, I know, that was a decade or more ago, but still I am bothered by the way things turned out."

"How is that, Dad? You told us you gave Bunny to a farmer—a good home, I remember you saying."

"Well, son, let me get around to the talk that the deputy sheriff had with me." He paused as if to give himself time to frame these thoughts. "The deputy said that I had to destroy the dog or give it away. But he told me bluntly that no one around Nelson would want a chicken killer. Once they get a taste of chicken blood, they never stop. It's pure instinct," he said.

"I promised I would take care of the situation." Father coughed again, holding his handkerchief to his mouth as if trying to render his admissions, like some sort of severe virus, harmless to others. "The following day when you were at school, I took Bunny out in the woods. Her eyes seem to plead, almost pathetically, as if asking for divine forgiveness and deliverance from her fate. It hurt every part of me—to end her life. I closed my eyes and I slowly pulled the trigger of the double-barrel. I shot her. Dammit, I shot her. I'm so sorry." Tears ran down his face, and I suddenly realized how much anguish he felt about Bunny's death. Now, looking back, I would describe his admission as almost a mortal wound to his soul.

"I forgive you," I said quietly, "both for what you felt was a necessary act and for the lie you told us." He gazed at me and reached for my hand, but we could not touch each other through the glass and steel bars that separated us.

"I guess this is where the story of Ol' Yeller ends," I told him ironically. "Don't all dog stories have a bittersweet ending?" I looked sadly at his face as the tears welled up in his eyes. "Dad, I guessed years ago that you probably had shot Bunny," I lied, partly to lessen his apparent pain. "This is not news to me, Dad. But if somehow you feel the need for my forgiveness, you have it."

"You know, son, it didn't all have to work out this way. Your life could have turned out differently."

"I know, it was my fault," I said squeezing out the truth that seemed to tighten my chest as if in a vice-like grip of something much larger. "All of it. After Bunny disappeared, I was so damn mad at that old bitch. Crazy mad, maybe. The feedstore where I had my part-time job kept rat poison in the warehouse. I stole a container, no big deal I remember thinking," I said lost in a trance of my own making. "I waited till all of you were asleep, then clambered over the chicken-wire. The rest was easy."

Father sighed, not from exhaustion, I suspected, but from a form of grief, I couldn't quite comprehend. "I have said it many times before, but the rat poison I mixed into old lady Larsen's chicken feed was meant for the damn chickens, not for her. I was too young and stupid to realize that the rat poison would make eating the chicken fatal—it never occurred to me that she would cook one of her dead laying hens. As for Alan's death—that was a tragedy that will always haunt me. How was I to know she would offer him a piece of her fried chicken?" I paused. "Not exactly the Colonel's chicken," I said, half-smiling.

Dad looked away as if in disgust at my jest. I could tell my father was not amused, but a part of me desperately needed to express some humor to lessen the deeply felt pain—both for him and for me—even if it was just unvarnished gallows humor.

Dad straightened in the hardback chair. "Robert, I will always be sorry that although you were a juvenile, you were tried as an adult. My heart will forever grieve for you. A life sentence seems so unjust." He pressed the palm of his hand against the glass, and I did the same, a touch without actually touching. I ached inside.

For a moment I was taken aback by the serenity I was witnessing in my father, perhaps at that moment he accepted that I would be alright in God's eyes, and he found some sense of release. Later this would fade as his depression worsened and the clouds of his mind turned grey.

"Dad, I have just one request of you. You know I feel incapable of praying, but tonight when you say your prayers, besides the obvious souls, please offer up a prayer for Bunny."

He stared through the prison glass that separated us and silently nodded.

As I write my final paragraphs of this brief but painful memoir, my today is a tentative beginning of another dreadful series of many never-afters. Like Michener's estuary, my prison days and nights slide by, as if I am incoherently speaking while neither awake nor asleep but in some state of animate existence somewhere in between.

I put pen to paper, tired, but feel impelled to finish.

Teach, that was the last year I saw my father, although on occasion I would get a letter. Cassie writes me periodically, and my twin brother, Duane, makes an annual pilgrimage to visit me, partly out of pity

I suppose, as he has a life of his own, which I truly understand. As for my other brothers, well, I guess in a sense I am dead to them.

In my father's last few visits, he seemed to change, a hollowing out that was almost palpable. It was a dark, dramatic transformation that subsumed the benign man of God I knew, and instead he seemed to retreat inside himself, as if a living tomb. Though Cassie never spoke of my father's emotional decline I often wondered if the lie he attributed to Bunny's death was an incomplete admission, the lie inconclusive; and that perhaps there were other more repugnant lies that he had chosen to conceal? Cassie once inferred that my father hid the truth well, but she refused to tell me more. I will never know. He died shortly after that. The warden adamantly refused my request to attend the funeral. I desperately wanted to be there, partly for my own sake and partly to make what I believed would be proper amends.

So much pain and so many deaths that my father had to endure: Cassie's mother, Delores, and his unborn child; my mother, and later, my dear brother Alan. I suppose I should also include old lady Larsen, though in some respects I don't feel sorry for her, although I am sure my father steeped in his piousness, would have grieved for her as well. In the end my father had to face his own faltering decline. Is that not the ultimate loss, even for a man of God? Life erodes to one's inevitable death. Admitting to me that Bunny's death had occurred at his own hands seemed to be the final straw. It is hard to imagine that the life and death of what many would consider a mere animal could have had such profound consequences for so many human beings—but that is the case. I try to remind myself that a dog is, after all, just a dog. I will never know whether my father's significant admissions and devastating losses, or his regrettable act of shooting a living, defenseless creature of God drove him to such utter despair. I will never know. But as he aged, the shadow of death seemed to descend on him like the haunting cliché of "a hungry wounded beast" and unhinged his troubled mind.

He told me before he died that his sins were an affront to God, and therefore unforgivable. I tried to argue otherwise, that what he had done was insignificant and that God forgives our sins, but he was not convinced. Perhaps, in the final analysis, the reason for his sin, or anyone else's sin, doesn't matter. Sins remain what they are, human fallibilities deeply entrenched in the subconscious mind; a sickness of sorts that many believe are only purged by prayer. I will never know whether he found a sense of expiation in his final days. I wonder if the state of atonement is—to use another cliché "a fool's errand" and an unattainable illusion.

Believe me, Teach, the cell block is dark, but as always never peaceful. I am physically and emotionally drained from this goddamn exercise. I intend to lay the pen down now and get some shut-eye. I wonder if the proverbial "silent slumber"—the last cliché that I feel impelled to write is from a children's lullaby; don't know. I believe it speaks eloquently only to the innocent and the virtuous—and I am neither.

"In her mind, the pony was a steed, a stallion perhaps, able to carry her away from her miserable existence."

VI

Woodsmoke

His ex-wife, now dead and gone, had sarcastically said that he dwelt in the past. He admitted to himself that at times, she had been perceptive; a bitch much of the time perhaps, but still, he admitted silently, perceptive.

"Bill, you could have had any professional occupation you wanted, but instead you had to be a damn social worker. There is a big L seared onto your forehead and it doesn't stand for luck." It stung like a red-hot brand, but was probably true.

William Martin sat uncomfortably on the custom log armchair he had crafted for his expansive chalet north of Nelson. His friends laughed when he called it a camp, but he tried to downplay his means. The chalet was set neatly back from the Net River, the fabled trout-fishing stream. The camp was a gift he had allowed himself after retiring from his position as the head of a social services department in the county.

He had detested the term "welfare office," as it was often referred to these days by the ill-informed political conservatives who now seemed to be running, or to his way of thinking, ruining the country.

He'd invested wisely over the length of his career, was financially comfortable, and had eagerly accepted the buyout that the Republican-run state legislature had given to the old guard. Now he spent his spare time flyfishing and grouse hunting in this remote area of the Upper Peninsula of Michigan.

Bill drew the Hudson Bay blanket up around this chest to ward off the harsh chill of winter's deepening evening. He knew his father, the late Pastor James Martin, or for that matter, Bill's equally conservative and uptight brother, the Right-Reverend Hank Martin Jr., would not approve of his plans, but as usual, he chose to do what he damn well pleased. He always had. As yet, Bill hadn't started a fire in the massive split-stone fireplace, partly out of apathy and partly because he was preoccupied with delusional ideations that had intruded into much of his life over many years. He recognized the pattern: first, the lack of adequate sleep; then the persistent negative thinking and racing thoughts; then periods of outright paranoia and vivid hallucinations. He, and his psychiatrist, understood that there was a hereditary component to the severe mental illness that had plagued him and other members of his family. He'd had these episodes many times before and he knew all too well that he was bound for what he often referred to as another crash and burn. These bouts had landed him in the psychiatric hospital several times over the course of his adult life. In moments of paranoia, the well-appointed living room seemed filled with specters, but the most vivid were the frightening hallucinations of Ellen, a young schoolmate long gone. Old ground, he fumed quietly to himself.

He'd majored in psychology at Michigan State University and knew that he was suffering once again from a mild case of psychosis, causing his reality to blur. Over the years he'd used the services of a psychiatrist, who would treat him with a low dose of an antipsychotic. The medication helped mitigate his paranoia and hallucinations. Mental illness was still a stigma, and as much as possible, he chose to keep his recurrences to himself. After several weeks of meds, he'd generally improve. His ex, who was not sympathetic, had branded him a nutcase. They had been married for twenty-five years before she'd walked. She'd passed several years ago and he hadn't grieved long. Now, without a lover and only one estranged son Bryan, he padded around the empty chalet in sheepskin slippers and a worn navy bathrobe. His son Bryan still blamed him for the many affairs he'd had during his parent's trying marriage, not understanding the complexities of his father's marriage to an obnoxious bitch. He saw little point in contradiction. He decided not to get dressed, he expected no company, and for that matter, didn't care.

He swept his greying hair out of his eyes. This evening's penetrating cold and his dread of the dark seemed to squeeze him in. His heart palpitated, a physical warning his doctor told him might happen as his chronic heart disease progressed.

Psychosis and chronic heart disease simultaneously, what luck, he dismally thought to himself. He'd experienced symptoms of each but rarely at the same time. Bill took little comfort in the prospect that he might succumb to heart disease. He lifted his etched brandy snifter and instead of his standard sip, drained the glass, then refilled his snifter from the crystal decanter he had conveniently positioned within reach on his coffee table. He knew where all this drinking was headed and accepted the inevitable.

He'd dealt with unpleasant hallucinations most of his adult life, although over the years the episodes had intensified. Bill knew he was unable to retreat from his psychosis after its onset and that the illness would have to run its course regardless of his choice of treatment. This, combined with the overpowering retrospection, was a curse that he had come to live with, like an ugly scar, a visible reminder of the past. Be that as it may, his insistent and vivid recall of a childhood schoolmate named Ellen caused him to suffer not only with regret, but with remorse as well.

He poured another brandy. The motion light came

on and he could see, through the gathering winter storm, a spike horn eating at the pile of feed corn outside his window. The young buck looked intently at the chalet, and perhaps sensing danger, with a flick of his tail bolted into the darkness of the nearby cedar swamp. Bill had put out extra corn today, expecting that tomorrow he might not be available to feed the buck.

Inebriated, and in the throes of his waxing psychosis, he agonized, suspecting that the memory would return; it always had—maybe half memory and half delusion, he wasn't sure. He floated into a disturbing recall. He'd been in the sixth grade—elementary school, in the isolated village of Nelson the day of JFK's assassination. Like everyone he knew, he recalled with vivid detail that fateful day; Ellen had cried openly. That was to be his first crucial recollection of Ellen, but certainly, not his last.

She was his schoolmate, not really a friend. She had a wandering eye, magnified by pointy cat's-eye glasses. The tips of the frames were inset with glittering rhinestones, some of which were missing from overuse and neglect. Her left eye darted around as if struggling to find a place where its owner could hide from her fellow classmates. The glasses had come from the local Lions Club, which collected discarded eyeglasses and gave them out to the poor. Unfortunately, the glasses, in combination with her severe shyness and simple looks, made her an object of derision by Bill and his fellow students.

Sixth-graders were often mean, and Bill was guilty of the crime of teasing and exclusion, though too young to understand his offense.

When teased, Ellen often giggled, hiding her crooked teeth behind her hand, as if a shield that she would use to stave off the ridicule that was a daily staple of her life.

Tall and gangly for her age, except for her gender, Ellen looked much like a scarecrow. Her long stringy hair was seldom washed, and she wore long cotton dresses even on the coldest days of the year, which were probably purchased from a Goodwill store. She lived many miles from the rural school, up in the conifer-covered granite hills miles from town.

She had a long ride to school in a poorly heated bus. Her family of four children and a disabled alcoholic father lived in a two-room tarpaper shack, with no running water or electricity. Bill's father, Pastor James Martin, made a pastoral visit once, but was put off by the unwashed drunken father.

Ellen always struggled academically and had been held back a year. One particular assignment stood out in Bill's mind. The students were required to present an oral report about a subject of their own choice. When it came time for Ellen to stand up in front of the class, several of the boys made rude comments and nasty gestures. She stood there and carried on, as if oblivious to the torment. The teacher did not intervene. Ellen's subject was the pony that a neighbor had given her. She spun a tale in which she and the pony rode through the woods, pursued by specters. The students had all laughed and mocked her fanciful notions. Only later in life did Bill understand the symbolism of her story. In her mind, the pony was a steed, a stallion perhaps, able to carry her away from her miserable existence.

And miserable it was. On Sunday, as the extended family had dinner, Bill's father had confirmed that Ellen did indeed have a pony. Sadly, he described the pony as a piteous creature roaming outside the family's squalid dwelling, its narrow ribs visible from lack of feed. "That poor creature is only fit for the glue factory," his father had said. Of course, the pony was not appropriately fed, as Ellen's family had difficulty even feeding themselves. Empathy being a painful lesson to learn, Bill had singled her out the following week, teasing her about her mighty stallion.

As a child, from his bedroom window across the street from the township hall, Bill would spot Ellen's family queued up for the monthly government food handouts of household staples, such as powdered milk, cheese, flour, and the like. Even if his father had not described the abject poverty of her home, it was evident to all, as Ellen always reeked of pungent woodsmoke, the acrid smell announcing that her family did not have enough means to afford fuel oil.

Ellen's only friend was a girl named Linda who was born with a cleft palate that, although repaired, had left her with a noticeable ugly scar and a pronounced lisp.

They could often be seen huddled together at lunch, eating cold sandwiches. Neither could afford the hot lunch. But they seemed to enjoy and value each other's company.

One winter's day on the school playground, he had pushed Ellen down in an icy snowbank. As she got up, her glasses cockeyed on her face, she had gazed at him, and whimpered, "Bill, why are you so mean to me?" Confused and unable to come up with a satisfactory reply, he'd just laughed.

She straightened her glasses, and from the magnified eyes, tears rolled down her face. Bill had turned away, his sense of shame a pain almost too great to bear.

He didn't fully understand that he might have wounded her, but in essence, she had killed him—or the only version of himself that he knew at the time. It was an epiphany, but at that time he didn't realize how his life as a human began at that very moment and would alter and evolve because of Ellen, and never be the same again.

There is sometimes dreadful power in memory, and the indictment he had seen in her eyes became his lasting memory of her. Over the years, during psychotic events he had been severely tortured by those memories. The eyes, the eyes—and the overpowering acrid smell of woodsmoke that seemed to assault his nostrils during his psychotic events were all that were left.

Ellen's life, Bill realized, had informed his own in

a whirl of thoughts, attitudes, and behaviors that he carried with him always, and if there was an afterlife, he would thank her for that. She was more than just a postscript to him, but had shaped his life as if a preamble of sorts. His education and vocation as a social worker had been prompted by Ellen in some sense, although when younger these volitions were subconscious. As an adult though, he began to understand their significance.

The local newspaper reported that when the tarpaper shack where Ellen lived caught on fire, she had rushed in to save her younger sister. They both perished.

Bill's father had given the solemn funerals, a quiet affair that bitter winter's day in 1964. Two simple pine caskets laid side by side in the quiet sanctuary. Very few people attended the graveside ceremony except her immediate family and Ellen's only friend, Linda, whom Bill comforted, his hand gently holding hers.

Bill poured another brandy; he supposed his last. The pain in his chest was excruciating and could no longer be denied.

"Ellen, will you give me the strength to…, I am frightened."

"Bill," he thought she replied, "come ride on my steed and we will fly like the wind." In his mind her eyes met his. The pain was almost unbearable. "Yes, Ellen I will come, I will come." He squeezed out the words and wheezed.

He pushed the rug up against the door to reduce any draft and although the flue was already closed, he jammed a pillow up the fireplace chimney for good measure. All that remained was to start a fire in the fireplace. The flames from the cedar kindling burst, sending sparks onto the fieldstone hearth, which he ignored. He set several sticks of seasoned maple on the fire and waited. Woodsmoke billowed all around him in the room, stinging his eyes as the familiar acrid smell assaulted his senses—but, he thought thankfully, not altogether unwelcome.

I am aware that you see me, Ellen. Your eyes; yes, Your eyes; and I ask for forgiveness.

Reviews of *North of Nelson Volume I*

...a magnificent portrayal of the bold rural life experiences in North of Nelson. The reader will certainly be captivated by this collection of short stories.

Mary C. Rajala

Retired L'Anse Area Schools

A very raw masculine perspective and a strong sense of place. His bittersweet, sometimes brutal stories, when read as a collection, span over a hundred years. He describes Northernmost Michigan, its remotely sparsely populated vastness, bringing it to life with the peculiar idioms of its inhabitants.

Ruth Ananda (Matthews)

Painter

Moore's writing has a charming flavor to it. The stories are riveting - you feel as if you're right there with his characters, sharing their experiences and emotions. Look forward to Volume II!

Hannah Eskel

I am privileged to have read North of Nelson Volume I by Hilton Everett Moore and anxiously await Volume II... I tumbled headfirst into his collection of short stories and was enthralled by his characters.

Trudi Rightsell

A well written tale...

Shane Haywood
Retired Police Officer

Moore's stories begin as a tightly woven fabric only to be unwoven as his characters come to life. Each of his stories entwine with another. He has an uncanny insight into the human condition and shows how each of us is a part of another. Moore shows how our actions are not truly actions of ourselves but rather a part of a chain reaction of love and hate, life and death in our universe.

Cynthia Dunn

...the stories take you on a journey and make you want to know more about each character. Good read!!!

Sue Manke

Hilton Everett Moore weaves a collection of short stories filled with beautifully flawed characters who are often unable to escape the consequences of their own poor decisions, and at times tragic circumstances.

David Beach

Moore's stories are reminiscent of Wendell Berry and Ron Rash where geography plays an important role not only in linking the stories but also serving as another character. While the location is distinctly the Upper Peninsula of Michigan, it transcends to other locations such as southern Ohio, eastern Kentucky, Appalachia, the Ozarks, or many other tight knit rural areas where family is paramount. The central theme of relationships draws the characters not only to each other but to the place they call home. Moore reveals the same affinity to the Upper Peninsula that he allows his characters to feel.

Robert Boldrey
M.A. in English, Professor
North Central Michigan College

These six stories reminds me of the early Joyce in Dubliners. Each is a careful analysis of deep and painful emotion generated by crime or illness or simply the remote ruggedness of Upper Michigan. I think a genuine U.P. literature needs this sort of work and am glad to see it.

Dr. Donald M. Hassler
Professor of English, Emeritus
Kent State University
Former Executive, Extrapolation
Advisor, International Authors Publisher

 **Hilton Everett Moore** is a published short story author who lives and writes at his remote cabin in the near wilderness of Baraga County in the Upper Peninsula of Michigan. He has held many positions in his life including: a stint as a kennel man for a Humane Society, a factory worker, later as a certified pipe welder in the oil fields of West Texas, also as an assistant manager of a lumber company. Ironically in a chapter he would like to forget, a gut-wrenching failed attempt at owning a restaurant. After a midlife crisis he went back to college and received a Master's Degree in Social Work. Upon graduation he was employed in the Michigan prison system as a Clinical Social Worker. Presently he enjoys writing in his cabin in the wilderness. He likes to fish with worms.

CPSIA information can be obtained
at www.ICGtesting.com
Printed in the USA
BVHW030928230223
659068BV00005B/135